"If your n... dressed to make him go gaga."

The familiar female voice was hidden in the darkness. "Or I'd slip on a little lacy number."

I peeked in the room to see if I had accidentally left the television on. I hadn't.

Jade Lee glowed in the darkness. There was a sparkling tiara like a cake topper on her head. "You should put on a tighter T-shirt. And your cheap bra kinda makes me sad."

I gulped.

Wisps of blond hair stuck out from underneath a pink turban that matched a long silk kimono loosely tied around her waist. She wore a pair of heels with a pink pom-pom on the open toe. The tiara glistened on top of the turban. "You can see me, can't you?" she asked.

Ahem. I cleared my throat and pretended not to see her.

No, no, no, the voice in my head begged. *Anyone but her,* the little voice kept talking to me.

Anyone but her. Anyone...

TONYA KAPPES

A GHOSTLY REUNION

A GHOSTLY SOUTHERN MYSTERY

WITNESS

An Imprint of HarperCollinsPublishers

Excerpts from *A Ghostly Undertaking, A Ghostly Grave, A Ghostly Demise, A Ghostly Murder* copyright © 2013, 2015 by Tonya Kappes.

A GHOSTLY REUNION. Copyright © 2017 by Tonya Kappes. All rights reserved. Printed in the United States of America. No part of this book may be used or reproduced in any manner whatsoever without written permission except in the case of brief quotations embodied in critical articles and reviews. For information, address HarperCollins Publishers, 195 Broadway, New York, NY 10007.

First Witness mass market printing: January 2017
ISBN 978-0-06-246695-2

WITNESS™ is a trademark of HarperCollins Publishers.
HarperCollins® is a registered trademark of HarperCollins Publishers.

16 17 18 19 20 QGM 10 9 8 7 6 5 4 3 2 1

*I have to say that my author bet was taken seriously
and I killed Jade Lee in a book! Thank you Jade
for being such a great sport! Thank you to reader
Cricket McGraw for winning the epitaph contest from
my newsletter! I'm beyond thrilled and love "gone to
the great pageant in the sky." Finally, to my family.
This has been such a crazy year! Six book deadlines,
Austin and Brady graduating from high school, and
Jack becoming a senior . . . .Eddy and my parents
(John Robert and Linda Lowry) have kept my family
going. And to Charlie, my wonder dog, who not only left
my side but continued to be so happy even after his leg
was amputated because of cancer. This year has been
amazing! All the love and support from my readers . . .
gosh . . . hand to chest . . . THANK YOU!!!*

XO~ Tonya

A
GHOSTLY
REUNION

Chapter 1

Sexy isn't a firm fanny in a thong, ladies." Hettie Bell didn't seem so sexy in her hot pink leggings and matching top as she gasped for breath in her downward dog position in the middle of Sleepy Hollow, Kentucky. Her butt stuck straight up in the air, right there on display for everyone to see. Her black, chin-length bob was falling out of the small ponytail on both sides and her bangs hung down in her eyes. "Sexy is confidence and self-acceptance. It's exactly what yoga provides."

Hettie Bell curled up on her tiptoes with her palms planted on one of the mats she provided for us. The rickety old floor of the gazebo, in the middle of the town square, groaned as we all tried to mimic her pose.

"Yes!" Beulah Paige Bellefry hollered out like we were in the first pew of the Sleepy Hollow Baptist Church getting a good Bible beating from Pastor Brown himself. "Amen to a good pose!"

Beulah continued to adjust her feet and hands each time she started to slip. If she wasn't a bit overweight, I'd say it was her eighties silk sweat suit that was slicker than cat's guts giving her problems. Or it could've been those pearls around her wrist, neck and ears weighing her down. Beulah never took off those pearls. She said pearls were a staple for a Southern gal.

"You said it, sister," Mary Anna Hardy gasped. She teetered side to side, nearly knocking into Granny. Her sweat left streaks down her makeup. Who on earth got up this early and put makeup on to do yoga? Mary Anna Hardy, that's who. "God help us!"

"That's it." I pushed back off my heels and crossed my legs, staring at all the Auxiliary women's derrieres at my eye level. "I'm here to do some relaxing, not Sunday school."

Sleepy Hollow was smack-dab in the middle of the Bible Belt and if God wasn't thrown in our conversations, then we weren't breathing. But the last thing I wanted to think about was my butt stuck up to the high heavens and everyone up in the Great Beyond looking down upon me.

Trust me, not a sight the living want to see at eight o'clock in the morning, either. Especially when I hadn't had my first cup of coffee for the day.

"Emma Lee Raines," Zula Fae Raines Payne, also known as my granny, gasped in horror. "Where are your Southern manners?" Granny's disgust of my behavior was written all over her contorted face.

My redheaded Granny only stood five-foot-four, but she was a mighty force to be reckoned with. At the ripe young age of seventy-seven, she'd give you the business while blessing your heart and pouring you a glass of her sweet iced tea no matter how mad you made her.

"My manners are right over there at Higher Grounds Café in liquid form in a large foam cup." I pushed back a strand of my brown hair that had fallen out of the topknot I stuck it in after I'd rolled out of bed when I decided to join the Auxiliary women and Hettie Bell for their morning yoga class. I needed my caffeine fix to wake my manners up.

"This reunion has helped you misplace them." Granny's disapproval of how I was handling the stress of planning my ten-year high school reunion showed in the creases around her tight lips, cocked brows and furled nose. "Doc said you need to take the necessary precautions to keep the 'Trauma' away, especially in times of extreme stress."

What did Doc Clyde know? Nothing.

"I'm sure you are stressed with no one to bury around here." Granny did a sign of the cross and we weren't even Catholic. She snapped her finger at me. "Now, downward dog, young lady," she ordered.

Doc Clyde, Sleepy Hollow's resident doctor, felt it necessary I do some type of stress relief since he had diagnosed me with what he called "Funeral Trauma" after I had gotten knocked out flat cold from a falling plastic Santa and woke up in the hospital seeing the clients I had stuck six feet in the ground. Being an undertaker can be stressful, but I didn't have "Funeral Trauma." I was a Betweener.

I saw dead people. Let me clarify, dead people that had been murdered. It was a gift that plastic Santa gave me. Unlike the annual ugly Christmas sweater Granny gave me, it was a gift that I can't return. Honestly, I wouldn't even be able to take the sweater back.

"It's okay, Zula Fae." Hettie Bell dipped back down into the stretch that started all this downward dog stuff. "Yoga isn't for everyone."

"You got that right," I grumbled under my breath and watched with a dutiful eye as the white convertible Mercedes whipped into a parking spot right in front of Higher Grounds.

Sleepy Hollow was a tourist town in Kentucky. We were known for our caves and caverns. Tourists to our town were mainly the outdoorsy type that loved to spelunk and stuff that I wasn't interested in doing. Now yoga was added to that list as well.

"Uh-un!" A woman jumped out of the convertible and wagged her hand at the car trying to park in the space behind her.

The woman had on a pair of big black sunglasses that took up nearly all of her thin face and a black scarf over her hair and tied under her chin. She wore a black strapless jumpsuit and her legs looked a mile long.

"Move!" she screamed at a car that was less desirable than hers. "You aren't parking that beater behind mine!"

She jumped into her car and backed it up, taking up the only two available spaces in front of the café.

"Is that?" Beulah Paige jumped up, tugged on the hem of her silky zip top and squinted.

"You know your fancy wrinkle cream might work if you got you some glasses or contact lenses." Mable Claire cackled and jingled all the way down to her mat.

"Oh, hush, Mable Claire," Beulah warned, keeping her eyes on the little scuffle going on in front of the café. "I do think that is . . ."

Beulah ran her hand over her bright red hair, pushing her fingertips in and fluffing it up. She put her hands on the strand of pearls around her neck and straightened them.

"Oh my God." Shock and awe came over me. Then anger when I saw who it was.

Jade Lee Peel.

I stood up to steady my shaking body. It took everything in my power not to throw one big hissy fit right there in front of all of Sleepy Hollow or at least the Auxiliary women.

"It is!" Beulah jumped up and clapped her hands together like a little schoolgirl, not the forty-something-year-old gossip queen I was used to seeing.

Beulah did a little two-step and giddyup down the steps of the gazebo and scurried across the town square.

"And it looks like Jack Henry is happy to see whoever she is too." Granny sure didn't know when or how to keep her mouth shut. Especially in an emergency such as this.

"Jade Lee Peel," I grumbled and gave my high school archnemesis the evil eye.

It was a time like this I wished I had some sort

of cool gift like casting spells on people, not seeing them after the spell took effect and stopped their beating heart.

Jade Lee had left Sleepy Hollow right out of high school to pursue a modeling career. When she made it on a music channel's reality TV show where they all lived in a house, she was discovered. She wasn't the biggest star on the planet, but she was the biggest from Sleepy Hollow.

Reluctantly I had sent her people an invitation to the class reunion hoping they'd think it was fan mail and when I hadn't gotten back an RSVP, I'd assumed she wasn't coming. It would be just like her not to RSVP and then make a grand entrance.

"I take it you aren't so happy to see her?" Hettie stood next to me with her hands on her hips and her leg cocked to the side.

Hettie Bell was lucky and didn't know just how evil Jade Lee Peel was as a teenager. Hettie had recently moved to Sleepy Hollow and opened up Pose and Relax yoga studio next to Eternal Slumber. She would've definitely been one of Jade's targets with her Goth girl look. Mary Anna Hardy down at Girl's Best Friend Spa tee-totally gave Hettie a complete makeover and turned her into a beauty right before our eyes with her new chin-length bob, super white teeth and minimal makeup. Not to mention that she already had a killer body from doing all that stretching and twisting she was trying to get me and the rest of the residents of Sleepy Hollow to do.

"Not in the least bit happy to see her." I couldn't take my eyes off Jade Lee. Her talons had hooked Jack Henry Ross, sheriff of Sleepy Hollow and my boyfriend, when we were in high school. And it seemed she was trying to hook him now, right there on the sidewalk in front of Higher Grounds Café. "She's the one who came up with my nickname, Creepy Funeral Home Girl, when I was in high school."

It was true. Kids could be so cruel. I was the butt of all their jokes. Granted, growing up in a family business was hard, but mine had to be the funeral home. My granny and parents were also undertakers and we lived in Eternal Slumber Funeral Home. Needless to say, I wasn't the most popular kid in school. Who in the world wanted to have a sleepover in a funeral home? No one. Least of all, Jade Lee Peel, the most popular cheerleader, prom queen and now small town celebrity. Even in high school she had celebrity status thanks to the community. After her mamma died of a stroke, Artie Peel, Jade's father and owner of Artie's Meat and Deli, did everything he could for his daughter, doing her no favors.

All the women in town felt sorry for Jade and

took her under their wing. I blamed the town for blowing up Jade's head as big as the town square.

"That's right." Hettie patted me on the back. "Your class reunion is this weekend."

"Yep." It was the only word I could muster up. My heart was breaking watching Jade and Jack exchange smiles, giggles, and whatever other else line of bull malarkey she was feeding him. No doubt trying to reel my handsome boyfriend into her lair.

Jade and Jack, their names were synonymous in high school. They even had their own nickname like Brangelina. JJ. Thinking about them with their own combined name made my stomach hurt and the feelings of the past flooded right back as if ten years had never passed. Only now I couldn't run over to my bedroom in the funeral home, slam my door and bury my head in the pillow.

"And you were in charge of the reunion, right?" Hettie reminded me.

I admit I almost didn't send Jade an invitation, but my good ole Southern manners, like Granny called it, won out. I can't say I didn't have a daydream about Jade coming back to town and seeing me in Jack's arms, but I certainly didn't daydream the other way around. I wasn't even on the high school reunion committee in high school, but the school called me since I lived here and asked me to put it together. Like Granny said, people were living longer, making funerals a little sparse. I had nothing better to do.

A white van with sketchy windows came plowing down the street and abruptly stopped right next to Jade and Jack. A bunch of men jumped out holding a big boom microphone and camera equipment.

Jade grabbed Jack by the arm and smiled as big as the day was long.

"Smile, Jack." I read her lips and heard her Southern twang in my head.

Jack fluffed up like a bandy rooster, sticking his chest out for all the world to see his sheriff's badge. The cameraman walked around them with the camera on his shoulder, taking shots from all angles.

"Yoo-hoo! Jade! Remember me?" Beulah waved and patted her chest. "Beulah Paige Bellefry! You used to play with these pearls in my Sunday school class." Beulah's grin took up her entire face. The balls of her cheeks squished up into her eyes.

Jade planted that sweet, fake smile across her face, giving Beulah a hug. Both of Jade's hands planted on the tops of Beulah's shoulders, giving her a pat on the left and then a pat on the right.

Jade's eyes grazed the grass along the town square, which drew them up to the gazebo. Our eyes caught. An easy smile was planted at the corners of her mouth. I glared at her, finding it almost impossible not to return her disarming smile.

She threw her keys to a young girl standing behind her. The girl ran in front of Jade and pulled open the door to the café, cowering down behind it. Her long brown hair was flat to her head. She had brown doe eyes and an olive complexion. She wore large black-rimmed glasses that were entirely too big for her face. But who was I to judge. I was by far no fashion expert. But it wasn't a surprise Jade surrounded herself with people who weren't as pleasing to the eye as she was. She always liked being the pretty one, center of attention.

I watched in horror as Jade grabbed Beulah's hand and tucked her other in the crook of Jack Henry's arm, dragging them both inside Higher Grounds. My heart sunk. My knees buckled. And any sort of Southern manners I had were thrown out the window.

"How do I look?" I ran my hand over my hair.

"Greasy." Hettie Bell's nose ruffled. She was never one to sugarcoat nothing.

I turned to Granny.

"Emma Lee, you are smarter than her. If dumb was dirt, she'd only cover about half an acre." Granny had her own way of trying to make me feel better.

I wasn't sure if she had just insulted me or had

given me a compliment. My head tilted, my eyes lowered and I stared at her.

"You are beautiful inside and out." Mable Claire jingled her way over. Mable Claire kept a lot of change in her pockets. She gave out dimes here and there to people who she passed on the street. "It's early, honey."

"Stop it." Hettie stepped up. "You are in workout clothes. She's gonna know you've been working out." Hettie jabbed my shoulder with her finger. "You are not the creepy funeral girl anymore. You are an important member of this town."

She was right. I wasn't that girl anymore and I had Jack Henry Ross now.

Granny scooted closer. She bent her lips to my ear. She smelled of cinnamon and sugar, easing my belly pain somewhat. She whispered, "Emma Lee, you go on in there and get your man."

I pulled back and we held each other's eyes for a second. I straightened my shoulders and stomped my way across the square and stood right in front of Higher Grounds.

I looked in the front window. Everyone inside was making a fuss over Jade Lee Peel being back in town, Ms. Sleepy Hollow herself, and everyone acted as if it were Christmas day. They were all crowded around her. Even little children who didn't know her, but knew of her and her legacy.

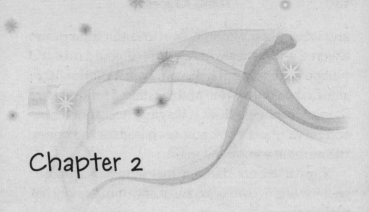

Chapter 2

"There you are." Cheryl Lynne stood at the door of The Watering Hole. "You hadn't come in Higher Grounds to get your coffee, so I thought I'd bring you a cup."

"You are the best." I put the high school reunion file down on the counter of the bar and walked over to get the cup. "I did try to come to get a coffee. In fact"—I paused to take a sip of the warm, welcoming brew—"I had my hand on the door handle, but it was so crowded, I left and decided to come here so I could make sure everything was ready for tonight's reunion kickoff."

Sleepy Hollow was a dry county, which meant there was no selling alcohol, at least in the legal way. There were a lot of people coming into town and I thought it would be fun to host a little pree-union get-together where everyone could mix and mingle. The Watering Hole was just on the other side of the county line and the only drinking joint around Sleepy Hollow. It was a perfect spot for everyone to come, relax and get reacquainted before the reunion tomorrow night.

"Crowded? Or the fact that Jade had dragged Jack in there?" she asked as if she didn't know the real truth.

"Both." I duck-billed my lips and sighed out my nose. I curled both hands around the cup. "Not that I don't trust Jack Henry, but when I saw her with him after all these years, it was like these past years had melted away. All the memories of her making fun of me and making out with him just flooded back, making me feel bad and I just couldn't make myself go in no matter how much Granny cheered me on."

"If it's any consolation, Jack wanted nothing to do with her." Cheryl's words did tickle my fancy a little. Enough for me to stand there and listen to more. "She has this camera crew with her and she was talking into the big camera all about her and Jack in high school and how they were royalty. Jack commented it was a long time ago and they were silly teenagers."

"He did?" My heart felt like it was growing in my chest.

"He did and he also got his coffee and left." Cheryl nodded. "But you aren't going to like this."

"What?" My voice fell flat, so did my heart.

"Mayor Burns came in." Her shoulders heaved up and down when she sucked in a deep breath. "And he told her he didn't know that she was coming into town and how he'd asked Jack to be the Grand Marshal of the parade in the morning, but he'd love it if she joined Jack because they were prom king and queen ten years ago."

It was like Lucifer had sucked himself up inside me. I could feel my blood starting to bubble up like a pot full of water on a lit gas stove, getting ready for the full rolling boil inside my body. I could feel the vein that ran along the side of my neck start to pulse its own heartbeat. My right eye twitched. Then my left eye twitched. My whole body started to twitch.

"Maybe you need to sit down." She grabbed my elbow and guided me over to one of the saddle seats that was a barstool. Gently she took the foam cup from my grip just before the lid was about to pop off. "I probably shouldn't have said anything." Her voice cracked.

"Oh, do go on." I held my finger in the air when

Hoss, the bartender and owner of The Watering Hole, walked by. "Shot. Maker's."

"Emma." Cheryl's voice held shame. "It's a little too early for a shot."

"It's either a shot of whiskey or a shot to Jade's pretty little head." My voice fell flat.

"Make it two." Cheryl lifted her hand and threw her leg over the saddle next to mine.

The bottle clinked when Hoss jerked the Maker's Mark from the bourbon shelf. He held the bottle on its side, giving a nice, long four-finger pour in one of the bigger shot glasses. He pushed the glasses toward us.

"Go hog wild." Cheryl held her glass up. I held mine up and we cheered.

"Lift 'em high and drain 'em dry," I said, bringing the glass to my lips as I threw back my head letting the smooth whiskey slide down my throat.

"Emma, is there anything else you need right now?" Hoss asked from behind the bar. "If not, I need to go out back and meet my vendors. They are here to drop off your wine cases and the other stuff you ordered."

"No." I looked back at him and shook my head. "I'm good for right now." I patted the glass.

"What are your plans?" Cheryl Lynne brushed back her long blond hair and pushed the glass aside.

"I thought I'd have the wine set up over there." I pointed over to the dartboard area near the front of the bar where the band would be set up. "Then over by the pool tables I figured would be the food table."

"Not here, I meant with Jade Lee." Cheryl Lynne had also been a classmate of mine. She was born with a silver spoon in her mouth and her daddy jumped at the chance of buying the old building in town square when Cheryl Lynne batted her eyes and told him she wanted a fancy coffee shop.

He even sent her to New York City to some sort of barista training. That was how we got Higher Grounds Café. I didn't mind Cheryl Lynne. She was sweet and harmless, and she wasn't mean to me in high school.

"Oh." I rolled my eyes and took another sip of coffee. "Her," I groaned.

"I just makes me sick how people fall all over her." Cheryl Lynne leaned up against the counter. "And to think she's now roped herself into riding with Jack Henry in Beulah Paige's convertible Cadillac for the parade."

Instantly I got mad at myself. Here I was letting Jade make me question my relationship with Jack, when I knew he loved me.

I ran my hand down my back pocket to make sure my phone was still back there and not in the car because I sure hadn't heard from him like I normally did in the morning.

"Jade Lee is a nobody to me or Jack Henry." I drummed my fingers on the counter.

"Sounds like jealousy," someone said from the door, their shadow dancing across the old wooden bar floor. The sun streamed in from behind them, blinding me to who it was.

I knew the voice, but didn't recognize the face.

"Ma'am, we are closed," Hoss said, hoisting a case of whiskey up on the bar top. He ripped the cardboard open and proceeded to fill his stock.

"Tina Tittle?" My eyes squinted to get a better look as if she weren't standing a foot in front of me. Or maybe I was digging back deep in my memory to recall the voice, but Tina's name popped into my head. She and Jade Lee were inseparable.

"The one and only." Tina twirled around with her hands out to her side. If I hadn't stepped back, her fingernails would've sliced me like a knife. "I knew it was you in here, Emma Lee, when I almost drove right past until I saw that damn hearse of your family's."

I let her comment roll off my shoulders. The hearse was a company car. I was in no shape or form going to spend money on a car when I could walk everywhere, mostly everywhere, I needed to go. Most of the time I only drove to pick up dead bodies, part of the job. Not a glamorous part of the job, but part of the job.

"What happened to your face?" It was like Granny said, this reunion had made me lose my manners. "I mean, you look different."

"That's what ten years out of a dumpy town like Sleepy Hollow will do for you." She patted her checks and trotted past me into the guts of the bar. "Not one teeny-tiny sip before I have to drive into that godforsaken town?" She pursed her lips at Hoss and flipped her red hair to the side.

"But your hair is red." Cheryl Lynne stared at Tina in amazement, noting how Tina's hair used to be blond like hers.

If I recalled, Tina Tittle used to put lemon juice in her hair and sit under a foil blanket during the summer to bring out what she called her "natural highlights." There was nothing natural on her now.

"Honey, you can have any hair color you want out in the real world." Tina dragged her finger down the bar, moving closer to Hoss. She put that finger in the air. "One, teeny-tiny sip." She winked.

"Emma, is she with the reunion?" he asked under his breath and looked at me from under his brows.

"She is," I said regrettably, leaving out the fact she and Jade Lee were inseparable in high school.

Not only was I going to have to deal with the one, I was going to have to deal with the two.

"What'll you have?" Hoss's tone had an edge to it. He was used to getting hit on every single night by women who came into the bar. It was old school for him and not even Tina Tittle was going to catch his eye.

"I'll have a little Elmer T. on the rocks." Her Southern accent dripped out of those plumped-up lips.

"So Emma Lee, you still hanging around the dead?" she asked, flinging her coffee-stained pant leg over one of the saddles. She eased up on the leather, putting her jeweled sandals in the stirrups and holding on to the horn.

"I have officially taken the reins from Granny." I reached for the shot glass, thinking about having another one. Then I realized that there was no amount of alcohol that was going to prepare me for this reunion.

Granny had retired from the funeral home business long after my parents did. They had up and moved to Florida while Granny stayed behind. She now owned and operated The Sleepy Hollow Inn, the only place to stay while visiting Sleepy Hollow.

She was booked to the gills this weekend and I was probably going to have to step up and help her since I didn't have any clients at either of my jobs.

In fact, summer was always a slow season for the dying. I wasn't sure why, but that was always how it had worked out. I didn't have any clients already six-feet deep bugging me either. It was actually kind of nice to feel a little normal, especially since my past few months had been spent trying to get ghosts to the other side.

"And you, little Miss Coffee." She turned her horns to Cheryl Lynne. Maybe not horns, but I swear if I was to part that fluffy long red hair, I'd find some sticking out of her head. "I see your daddy came through. Again." Sarcasm dripped from her mouth.

Hoss slid the glass down the bar, landing it perfectly into Tina Tittle's hands. She grinned and pulled the drink up to her lips, taking the tiniest sip I'd ever seen in the sexiest of ways. The big diamond rings across her hand sparkled even in the dark bar.

"You heard." Cheryl was much nicer than I was feeling.

Granny was right. This reunion has stripped me of all my filters and sent my manners out the window.

"Of course. Jade Lee was so excited to see there was a real coffee place in town. Unlike the Buy-N-

Fly." She cackled before throwing her head back and letting the entire glass of whiskey slide down her throat. "Speaking of, I'm meeting Jade at Girl's Best Friend for a spa day." She threw her leg back over to get off the saddle. She walked past me and wiggled her fingers over her shoulder. "Toodles."

Cheryl Lynne, Hoss and I stood there with the silence hanging between us, unusual for a honky-tonk bar.

Hoss broke the silence.

"I'll bet you a hundred dollars those girls are up to no good," Hoss challenged me. I was too smart to take a bet from a bookie.

"I'll bet you're right." I sucked in a deep breath and kept my eyes on the door, knowing deep down something bad was about to happen.

Chapter 3

"Welcome to Hardgrove's." The young receptionist sat at a half-moon desk in the reception area at Hardgrove's Legacy Center. "How can I help you today?" she asked with a sweet smile on her face.

A soothing jazz number piped through the sound system made me feel a little less stress than I'd had driving here. There was a waterfall in the center of the room behind the receptionist desk, adding to the ambiance along with a sitting area with leather chairs and examples of what types of urns families could purchase for the ashes of their loved one.

"I'm here to see Charlotte Raines." My sister was

the funeral director of this particular location of Hardgrove's.

We'd known the Hardgroves all of our lives. They too grew up in the funeral home business. We spent all of our vacations together, even though none of us wanted to. During the summers my parents would drag us to funeral conventions and call it a family vacation. Some vacations.

Charlotte and I would spend most of our time in the room or in the hotel arcade room if they had one. We'd see the Hardgrove kids and felt like kindred spirits because they were in the same boat as us.

There were three Hardgrove kids, Gina Marie, Dallas and Darrin.

Their funeral homes had never been in direct competition with us since they were located in several areas of Kentucky—Sleepy Hollow not one of them.

But the day Charlotte Rae left Eternal Slumber to move to Lexington and took up employment with the Hardgrove's was the first time I'd seen Granny almost needing to be stuck in one of them mental facilities. She about lost her good Southern mind. It was unheard of to leave a family business for someone else's family business in the same industry. Charlotte Rae not only made our family look bad, it made our business look bad.

Charlotte Rae hem-hawed around about how Hardgrove's was the new way of funeral home services. A legacy center. Now I could see what she was talking about.

"Do you have an appointment?" the girl asked as her finger scanned down what looked to be an appointment book of some sorts.

"I'm her sister. I wouldn't think I'd need an appointment to see family." I glared at the girl.

She obviously didn't know how to act in a small town, not that Lexington was all that small, but still she was living here and should've known that you didn't need an appointment to see someone.

The girl grabbed the phone and punched in some numbers.

"Do dead people ring you up and tell you they are about to die and their family will be contacting you?" I grumbled under my breath. My patience had been worn thin and I was hoping to find some sort of comfort in talking to my sister.

"Emma Lee"—Charlotte Rae emerged from someplace behind the water fountain—"I'm so glad you are here."

I looked over at the girl. Her head was already buried into something else on her desk.

"Are you here about that old colonial inlaid sideboard?" Charlotte was dressed in an emerald green suit. It matched her long red hair and fair skin perfectly. I glanced down. My sweatpants and sweatshirt probably weren't what I should've worn here, but it was on a whim that I had come.

"The sideboard in the entrance of Eternal Slumber?" I asked, a bit confused.

"Or not." She crossed her arms and curled her perfectly manicured nails around her arms.

Of the two of us, Charlotte Rae had been dipped in the better end of our gene pool. She needed little effort to look as good as she did. I, on the other hand, had to get by with some makeup and good manners. She was the pretty one; I was the nice one. At least that was how people referred to us when we were growing up.

I'll never forget the one time we were teenagers and helping in the funeral home and an old geezer came up to me. He said, "Your sister Charlotte Rae sure did get your Granny's good looks. Emma Lee, you are just like your daddy. Awfully sweet."

I wasn't sure, but I think it was an insult.

"What about the sideboard?" I asked. No amount of softly playing music was going to take this stress away.

Charlotte Rae's eyes shifted. "Have you taken your medication lately?" she asked.

"Don't give me that," I warned. She and Granny were always on me about the little pill Doc Clyde had prescribed for me to help keep the crazies away since they thought I had the "Funeral Trauma." "You tell me what you are talking about."

She opened a door and stepped inside. It was the biggest office I had ever seen. The sun swirled in the reception area from the large windows and I swear the bright light created a nice little halo around pretty little redheaded Charlotte Rae.

"Can I get you something to drink or eat?" she asked, using her good manners.

"No." I had come to get some big-sister advice on how to deal with the reunion. The sideboard comment had thrown me off guard and I was about to pounce. The soft music was really pleasant and drew me out of my thoughts. "Maybe I should play music at Eternal Slumber."

"On that old sound system." Charlotte Rae harrumphed. She was right. The volume button on the sound system at Eternal Slumber had to stay between the numbers three and four. If the knob was under three, there was no sound. And above four it was crackly.

"It's a thought." I shrugged, not completely discounting the possibility of having music play. Of course I'd have to check the budget and see if it's even financially possible. That had been Charlotte's job before she left me high and dry. She was in charge of all the financials of Eternal Slumber while I took care of the arrangements by making sure everything went as planned.

"This sure is a fancy place." I looked around, trying not to sound so envious.

She laughed. "It truly is the way of the future. A legacy center. I told Granny that you two should think about opening something like this on the outskirts of town."

"Granny says there is nothing fittin' about having baptisms, wedding showers and funerals all under one roof." No matter how much I tried, I couldn't get Granny to come see Charlotte at Hardgrove's. Not even a bribe worked. "Besides, Granny said that old man Hardgrove was probably rolling over in his grave at what his grandchildren have done."

When in fact, what the grandchildren had done would likely have quite the opposite effect. Hardgrove's Legacy Center wasn't just a funeral home. Gina Marie Hardgrove being the driving force, not to mention the brains, behind the new and improved funeral home business.

"Or he's laughing all the way to the bank." Charlotte shrugged.

Hardgrove's had opened up what Gina Marie called Legacy Centers all over Kentucky. They were nice big buildings with several different conference-type rooms. It was the darndest thing

I'd ever heard. The Legacy Center wasn't just for funerals; people could rent out the rooms for all sorts of stuff. They even had party planners, but not Charlotte Rae. She was strictly the undertaker of this location and only handled the funerals.

"Let's get back to the sideboard." I was curious to see what she was talking about.

"It's nothing." She batted her hand at me. "I'm sure Granny will discuss it with you."

"I'm right here." My head tilted to the side. The big diamond on her middle finger about blinded me. I used my finger and gestured between us. "Why don't we just talk about it right now."

"I was going to let Granny handle it, but if you insist." She smiled and flailed that diamond in the air. Charlotte Rae had a way of flaunting without actually saying it out loud and waving her hand around like a flag on a windy day was her way of showing off the big rock. "Granny always said the sideboard was mine and I'd like to go ahead and take it."

"Take it?" I asked, swearing she'd just aged me ten years. She nodded her pretty little head up and down. "Take it? As in away from Eternal Slumber?"

There wasn't a time I could recall that the sideboard wasn't sitting where it was sitting today. Even when my mamma had the carpet pulled tight. "Don't be going and moving the sideboard," Mamma told the carpet men. "It's bad luck to move key pieces of furniture in a funeral home." The sideboard had been there long before I was and was a beautiful antique.

"You honestly think that Granny is going to go along with it? And me?" I pointed to myself.

"It is mine." Charlotte folded her arms and curled her hands around her biceps.

"When Granny is dead!" I banged my hand on Charlotte's desk. Instead of shaking the sting out of my hand, I fisted it. "And she's nowhere near being stuck in the ground."

I was so mad, I had forgotten what I'd come here for. I stood up; Charlotte did too. I stalked out of her office and down the hall.

The thought that Charlotte would want her inheritance before Granny was dead infuriated me. Charlotte and I were definitely not cut from the same cloth. She was always worried about her appearance, which was probably put on her by the community—everyone always telling her how pretty she was, while my greatest compliment was how nice I was. I'm sure it was hard for Charlotte to live up to her God-given looks all the time.

I turned and faced the sliding entrance doors.

"By the way," I jerked my head around once I reached the front of the building. "I didn't insist,

I suggested we talk about the sideboard. I merely suggested it since I was here. Now I regret it."

"Cremated." Charlotte's chin dipped; she stared at me with those green eyes.

"What?" My face contorted. I glared at her.

"Granny's wishes are to be cremated." She smiled with cruel confidence.

My mouth opened. I snapped it shut. Turning on the balls of my feet, I marched out the door and slammed it behind me.

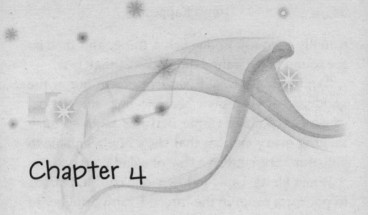

Chapter 4

How could you?" I stomped around the kitchen of the Sleepy Hollow Inn. "It's an Eternal Slumber heirloom. Not just a family one. It's a staple in the Sleepy Hollow community. Everyone in the community always comments on it. And cremation? Since when did you want to be charred like a pig from a pig roast?"

Granny planted her fists on her hips. Her face as red as her hair. She might be only five-foot, four-inches, but she still put the fear of God in me.

"Are you done showing yourself?" Granny's brows cocked. Her disapproval of my behavior showed on her face.

"Maybe." I wasn't able to commit to definitely being done. I was so mad that Charlotte Rae would actually even ask to do such a thing, and that, by the sound of it, Granny didn't discourage her.

"And here I thought you came here out of the goodness of your own heart to help me out because God knows Hettie Bell has been so busy making everyone Zen that she's not been able to help out." She shoved a tray of salad plates at me.

When Hettie came to town, she couldn't afford to pay for a room in the Inn so Granny put her to work and let her live there for free. After Hettie opened Pose and Relax, she continued to work part-time and help out Granny when she could. Granted, Sleepy Hollow Inn wasn't generally as busy as it was now since it was reunion weekend.

Granny's eyes snapped up.

"Take this to table three and come back. We will talk then." Granny was good at laying the guilt trip on me.

Granny pushed it toward me again. Reluctantly I took it. She was as stubborn as a mule and I knew if I didn't deliver the salads to the customers in the Inn's dining room, Granny wasn't going to tell me a thing about the conversation she had with Charlotte Rae about the sideboard.

I gripped the black tray, holding it close to my gut. I turned and headed toward the swinging kitchen door, knocking it open with my backside. Laughter spilled out into the hallway of the Inn.

Granny had really made the Inn very cozy for the guests. She even opened the dining room up as a restaurant for the community. There was nothing better than Granny's home cooking.

There was not a single table open in the dining room. I kept the tray steady and headed straight for table three. It was the most requested table. It sat on the backside of the Inn next to the large window with the best view of the mountainous caves that put Sleepy Hollow on the tourist map.

I put the tray above my head and curled up on my tiptoes to get past the extra chair the patrons had added to the two-top table to make it a three top.

"You can't get through there?" The voice sent chills up my spine as it raked up my body like nails on a chalkboard. "I mean, there is a lot of room. Scoot up, Mary Anna."

I sucked in a deep breath and lowered the tray.

"Who had the Cranberry Cave salad?" I asked, ignoring Jade Lee Peel. It was convenient how Granny left out the little detail the salads were for Jade and her group.

"Me." Tina Tittle twinkled her fingertips in the air. "Emma Lee has really done a great job for tonight's get-together at The Watering Hole."

I smiled at Tina. She was never as mean as Jade, but she didn't have a spine.

"Who had the Chicken Cobb Cave?" I asked.

Mary Anna Hardy stuck her hand up in the air. It took everything I had not to flip the salad on her Marilyn Monroe styled head of hair.

How could she? I made eye contact with her and glared. Her eyes popped open and she gave a slight shrug.

Mary Anna owned Girl's Best Friend Spa and was the beautician for my clients at Eternal Slumber. I never understood why she loved doing hair for the dead, but she did.

"Stalagmite Spinach Salad, no salt?" I asked, wishing I had a real stalagmite to stab Jade Lee right in the heart.

There was really no need to ask who had the spinach salad. Jade Lee was known to order everything without salt. She claimed it made her puff up like a big balloon and made her eyes have dark circles.

"Me." Jade looked at me with a hard, cold-eyed smile. "The Watering Hole." She rolled her eyes. Her nose curled. "I've never been fond of smelly bars. But if it's the best you could do." She picked up her fork. I resisted grabbing it and stabbing her in the neck. She moved the spinach around on the plate. She leaned over to Tina. "At least she didn't plan it in the creepy funeral home."

A giggle escaped their lips. A tightening of anxiety crept in my heart sending me back in time to high school and Jade's cruel, underhanded remarks for me every time she saw me. Tina glanced up at me; a melancholy frown flitted across her features.

"Will that be all?" I asked, using the manners Granny taught me to use. I dropped the tray to my side.

"Thank you, Emma Lee." Mary Anna touched my arm. "Tell Zula Fae it looks delicious. And it's so nice of you to take time out of your busy day to help her." She nodded toward the other girls.

"I'll be sure to tell her." I bit my lip to stop me from saying something I'd regret.

I made sure I looked around on my way out of the dining room to see if anyone needed refills. Whispers of the homecoming parade fluttered through the dining room. It was exciting.

Before I walked out, I turned back around and took a nice long look at Jade Lee Peel. She might have been the homecoming and prom queen when I was in school and had the best clothes, but I had the best accessory. Jack Henry.

"Granny, why didn't you tell me that tray was for Jade Lee?" I asked after I bolted through the kitchen door. Granny stood with her back to me. Her arms were going back and forth in a rapid motion with her rolling pin.

"If I did, you'd probably spit in her spinach."
Granny laughed her wicked laugh.

"You are right about that." I set the tray on the
kitchen table. "Oh." I reached over to the basket of
fresh out of the oven biscuits.

"Ah . . . ah . . ." Granny tsked. She put the rolling pin down and wiped her hands on her apron.
"That's for table three."

"No way am I going back out to table three."
I shook my head. I cleared my throat like I was
going to bring up a big mucus ball ready to spit
on them.

"She ain't worth the salt I put in that bread."
Granny winked and pushed the bread basket
across the table.

"You didn't." The biggest grin crossed my lips.
I grabbed the basket. "I'll be right back and when
I am, we are going to talk about that sideboard."

I hurried back out to table three and slipped the
basket on the table while they were in deep conversation about hair and hair color. Happy they
didn't seem to notice. Happier when Jade Lee took
a biscuit and bit her pretty, pearly white teeth
down into the fluffy dough.

"Mary Anna is a traitor." I plopped down at the
kitchen table. Granny put a hot biscuit in front of
me and slid the butter dish over.

The knife cut through the room temperature

butter like a warm, comfort feeling. I spread the butter on and ignored Granny's stare as I took a bite. I closed my eyes and took in the sweet, savory dough.

"You are going to have to let that girl be if you are going to enjoy yourself." Granny tapped the table with her finger. "You are the one with the prize."

"Jack Henry is a prize." I held the last bit of biscuit up to my face and sighed with happiness. Jack Henry and butter biscuits were two things I thoroughly enjoyed in life.

"No matter what you do, that girl is always gonna be like a bugger you just can't thump off." Granny eased down onto the seat across from me.

"No matter how much you try to make me feel better, every single time I look at her, I think about her calling me the creepy funeral home girl." I slumped down in the chair.

It was funny how those feelings of sadness swept over me like it was yesterday.

"And this whole sideboard isn't making this any better," I grumbled.

"You know Charlotte Rae," Granny declared. "She's always been a little big for her britches. I would've given it right to her if she'd stopped by and made a visit. She called and asked for it."

Granny and I both knew that around here, if you

wanted a favor, or in Charlotte Rae's case, a family heirloom, you made a visit, not a phone call.

"So you aren't giving her the sideboard?" I questioned Granny with hope in my heart.

"Not anytime soon." Granny winked and pushed herself up to her feet. "Now, you run along and be sure that you are all prepared for this evening and tomorrow. Make sure everything goes off without a hitch." She shook her finger at me. "That way little Miss Priss can't say a dag-gon word about you. Ever."

"Who might this Miss Priss be?" Marla Maria Teater stood at the screen door in the kitchen in all her glory with Lady Cluckington attached to a dog leash around her wrist. She wore a skintight black dress that hugged her curves more than the pavement on the back roads. Her red high heels matched her red lips.

"Don't you think you are bringing that fowl in here," Granny protested, and snapped the hook lock on the door frame. "Or I'll wring its neck and pluck it clean." Granny licked her lips. "Mmmm, mmmm. I can taste that prize chicken now."

"You have lost your mind, Zula Fae." Marla Maria grabbed Lady Cluckington and tucked her under her armpit. "You think that little lock is going to keep us out?" Marla Maria clucked.

"Hi there." I got up and flipped the hook up, letting Marla Maria and Lady Cluckington in. "It's been a while since I saw you."

We gave each other a quick hug. I patted Lady on the top of her head.

"Are her nails painted?" I asked, noticing Lady's pink claws.

"Doesn't she look great? Precious pink just like mine." Marla twinkled her hand up in the air. The same color nail polish on her nails.

Granny snarled and mumbled a few unintelligible words under her breath before she went back over to the stove and stirred whatever she had in the pots.

I hadn't seen Marla Maria since her deceased husband, Chicken Teater, had become a Betweener client and haunted me until I figured out who killed him and had it out for his prize chicken, Lady Cluckington. Thankfully, with the help of Chicken and Jack Henry, Chicken had happily crossed over and his murderer was in jail.

"Honey?" Marla Maria stepped back and squinted. "You look tired. Have you been using that Preparation H like I told you?" She reached out and patted skin underneath my eyes.

"I had heard Jade Lee Peel was in town and I just had to get in front of her." Marla Maria had on a full face of makeup.

"Why?" I asked flatly, knowing exactly why she was here and dressed to the hilt.

"It would be great for business if I had an endorsement from her." Marla Maria picked up Lady and stroked her feathery body. "After all, I do run the only pageant school around and she is the face of Sleepy Hollow," she squealed with delight. "Here." She shoved Lady against me. "You don't mind watching Lady while I just go peek in the dining room, do you?"

Whether I minded or not, Marla sashayed out of the kitchen, twisting and turning as if she were on the pageant runway.

"Get that varmint out of here." Granny's arm jerked out and her finger pointed. She meant business.

I nearly knocked Mary Anna down when I rushed out the front door with Lady Cluckington tucked in the crook of my arm.

"Lady Cluckington." Mary Anna laughed and patted Lady on the head.

I set her down in the front yard and held on to her leash while she stabbed her beak at anything and everything on the ground. I could only imagine Chicken Teater going crazy watching me from the Great Beyond—he never let Lady eat anything that he wouldn't eat.

"Marla Maria made a beeline for Jade, giving

me the signal to get out of there," Mary Anna said.

"And why were you with that snob?" I tried to hold back from the gossip, but it was too much for me to hold in. I was like a shaken up Coke can, ready to explode once opened. Mary Anna opened me. "You are my friend. Not hers. She is evil and mean to me."

"Geesh." Mary Anna grinned from ear to ear. "Little Miss Emma Lee has a dark side."

"I do not," I protested. Then I corrected myself. "She brings it out in me."

"Her hair stylist can't fly into town because of some family emergency, so she's asked me to do her hair and makeup while she's here." Mary Anna rolled her eyes. "She and Tina and . . ." Mary Anna tapped her temple. "I can't remember that assistant's name, but anyways"—she shooed off the minor slip of memory—"they came into the shop to buy out a few hours for me to do her hair."

"Oh, yeah. Tina said something about that this morning." I recalled her saying something about it at The Watering Hole, but didn't get all the details because I was so shocked by her appearance and too busy taking it all in. "Thank God you aren't doing her hair." I let the leash out a little more so Lady could continue to eat up whatever was in the grass.

"Oh, yes I am." Mary Anna's chin flew up in the air and down again. "She's paying me some good money and with no clients from the nonbreathing, it will make up for the lack of business from the Grim Reaper."

"You are not only a traitor, but you're sick." I couldn't help but laugh. "You've been Jaded," I groaned.

"I've been what?" Mary cackled. "Jaded?"

"Yep. It's what Charlotte Rae and I used to say when everyone in town used to drool all over Jade when she was in high school." I shook my head. "They were all jaded by her good looks and overlooked her evilness."

"Oh, Emma." She batted at me. "I've got to get going." She turned and waved behind her back. "She has a specific hair color she uses on her hair and she gave me the formula. I have to go make some up because she will be over shortly to get her hair and makeup done for tonight."

"Tonight," I growled under my breath. I had absolutely nothing to wear that would compare to how Jade would be dressed.

Tonight was going to be a disaster. I could feel it.

"Ms. Hardy!" The girl called from the top of the Inn steps, flailing her arms in the air. "I'm coming with you!"

I jumped out of the way, tugging Lady Cluckington's leash, almost strangling her to death. Lady's wings flew up in the air sending feathers flying when the girl ran past.

"Pfft. Pfft." The girl spit and waved her hand in front of her to detour the feathers from flying into her mouth.

Mary Anna stopped on the sidewalk. When the girl got closer, I could tell it was the same girl that had opened Higher Grounds Café's door this morning for Jade and Jack.

I grabbed the leash and hurried to the tree where Granny kept her moped tied up to listen in on their conversation. The girl knew Mary Anna; Mary Anna apparently knew the girl, but I didn't. In and even around a small town like Sleepy Hollow, I knew and had heard of everyone.

"Really you don't have to come." Mary Anna's head bobbled. "I've been a hairdresser for many years and I know what I'm doing."

"I've been Jade's assistant for many years and I know how she can be." The girl's tone turned cold as she warned Mary Anna. "And if you don't get it right, I'm telling you that this career you have been doing for many years"—the girl gulped—"will be over."

I wondered what exactly she did for Jade. She was as plain as the day was long.

"There you are." Marla Maria clomped down the Inn's front steps in a manner less than pageant style. Her strides were stiff and her hands balled up in fists. "I hope my Lady didn't eat something bad for her." She jerked the leash from my hand and bent down to pick up Lady. She stroked her body. "After all, she is a prize hen."

"Take it easy," I assured her. "Lady is just fine. What got up in your nest?"

"That . . . That." Her lips pinched. Her eyes snapped open. "That. That," she pointed at the Inn with her finger, "so-called beauty queen! Argh!" She shook her head and tucked Lady up under her armpit before she stomped off.

"I guess asking her to be your spokesperson didn't go so well," I muttered under my breath, and watched Marla Maria. She was so mad. She was shaking like a hound dog trying to get at the squirrel it treed. "And that's what Jade Lee Peel does to you."

I shook my head. In forty-eight hours Jade Lee would be out of here and life in Sleepy Hollow would return to normal. Unfortunately, Jade Lee could do a lot of damage in that forty-eight hours. I'd seen it all my life.

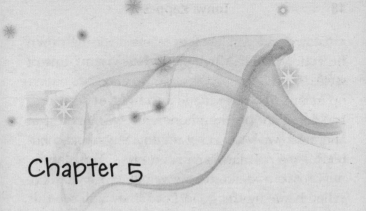

Chapter 5

Business was down. Not many people were dying, which was good for the community but not for paying bills. I had spent so much time working on the reunion over the past few weeks that I had let the premade funeral arrangements go to the wayside.

Some people thought it was creepy to think about their own funeral arrangements before they died, but it was a blessing for the family. I'd seen it so many times where the family was grieving so much, they were unable to make decisions of sound mind, or they wanted to give their loved one a wonderful send-off but found they couldn't afford to do so.

With premade arrangements, the loved one had

already decided what they wanted for their own funeral. Morbid? Maybe, but that was my line of work.

"I think you have made a wonderful decision," I told a client on the phone who was coming in later next week to get set up on a payment schedule for his premade arrangements. "Your family might not understand now, but when you are called home by the good Lord, they will see this was a blessing in disguise."

I wasn't beneath using the Lord's name when it came to business. After all, Sleepy Hollow was in the Bible Belt and we did love our Baptist religion. Anytime the Lord's good name was used, people took notice. It was the way of life here. Two things we took serious: religion and politics. Other than that, it was all gossip.

The light rap on my office door caused me to look up. Fluggie Callahan stood at the door with her blue knit shirt tucked plum down in her pants that were pulled up plum under her armpits. A long red scarf circled her neck and hung down in front of her.

"I'm glad you are here." Her eyes bore into me from under her Coke-bottle glasses perched up on her nose causing her white eyelashes to jump out even more. Her sandy-blond hair was pulled up in the normal scrunchie and bobby pins stuck all over the base of her head kept the stray hairs from falling down. "I need the scoop on Jade Lee Peel." She plunked a file on my desk bigger than the phone book. "And from what I understand, you are in charge of the class reunion, which means you know her because you went to school with her."

"What scoop?" I asked, and leaned back into my chair.

"The reality show." Fluggie pushed the file across my desk.

Fluggie was the owner, editor and reporter for the *Sleepy Hollow News*. We had worked together a few times when I needed some insider information for one of my Betweener clients and her journalism sleuthing skills came in real handy. Of course she didn't know about my Betweener job and by the looks of things, that job had come to a complete stop. I was happy to say that no ghosts of any type had visited me and I couldn't be more thrilled.

"Reality show? You mean the show she was on years ago when she moved away from Sleepy Hollow. That music channel's reality show?"

"No, I mean the one that's all hers. The one the camera crew is here for." She tapped her fingernail on the file.

My jaw dropped. "So"—I opened the file— "that's what that film crew was all about."

"You saw the film crew? They are already filming then." Fluggie pulled out her notebook and wrote something on it. "When did you see them?"

"This morning." I skimmed the pages Fluggie had in the file. Most of them were pictures from the internet Fluggie had printed off, but one caught my eye. I took it out of the file. "I was doing yoga with the Auxiliary women when she rolled into town with a film crew taping her every move. She was going into Higher Grounds. I'm sure Cheryl will be more than willing to tell you about it if she's going to get some free press from you."

"From what I gathered, the filming wasn't set to begin until the night of the reunion." Fluggie shrugged.

The thought of Jack Henry on her arm as she walked into the café burned me to the core. I didn't want the world to see my boyfriend on her arm. That would make a mockery out of me, which was not only bad for business, but bad for me.

From what I gathered, without reading, the article was about Jade Lee signing on to do a reality TV special about what it was like to be a hick from a small town and growing into a swan.

"Hick?" My voice escalated. "She was far from a hick. She is going to make us look like some backward town."

"If she features Sleepy Hollow, our economy

might just get a bump." Fluggie smiled. "I'd love to get the scoop from her and get my article online before anyone else and let it go viral. That's why I'm here actually."

"I'm not following." I put the article down on the desk. "What do you want from me?"

"I want you to get me an exclusive." Fluggie set her pen and paper on the edge of the desk and crossed her arms.

"Are you kidding me?" I shook my head. I muttered, "This town has gone nuts."

"You owe me." Her brows raised; her head slightly tilted to the right. "I got you all that information on Cephus Hardy and those other dead people."

"If you remember"—there was no way I was going to let Fluggie hold some little bits of information over my head—"I paid that debt by getting the council to reopen the newspaper."

When I first needed Fluggie's help, the *Sleepy Hollow News* had gone under and she'd been working at another paper. Long story short, I got the council to approve the newspaper and Fluggie had a job running it.

"You forget I write all the obits and lately I've noticed Burns Funeral Home"—Fluggie reminded me of Eternal Slumber's number one competition—"is getting a lot of bodies, not to mention press in the paper when they are having viewings."

How could she? I glared at her. Fluggie was good at hitting below the belt.

"I want a free ad as big as a page." I straightened my shoulders. "And I want you to write up a really nice article about Eternal Slumber and premade funeral arrangements and how important those are. And . . ." My little brain was working overtime. "I want you to do an exclusive on the whole reunion weekend starting with The Watering Hole tonight with a photo of Jack Henry Ross and me coming into the bar, arm in arm."

"Like a societal page? Who's Who in Sleepy Hollow?" She pondered.

"Yes." I snapped my fingers. It would be like an announcement for my relationship with Jack Henry.

"Deal." Fluggie Callahan stuck her hand out. I took it. "Only if you get me a sit-down face-to-face, pictures and all."

"Now you're pushing it." There was a churning in my belly. I knew I was going to regret it. The last thing I wanted to do was ask a favor from Jade Lee Peel.

Within a few minutes, Fluggie was gone and I
was heading out the front door of Eternal Slumber.

The sun was shining and the birds were chirping.
There was no denying Sleepy Hollow was going
to have great weather not only for the parade tomorrow morning, but the entire reunion weekend. It sure did seem like Mother Nature was
helping me.

A flurry of activity was going on in front of the
square with people gathered around, moving like
a wave away from the town square. Jade Lee Peel
emerged from the crowd right in front of Girl's Best
Friend Spa, where Mary Anna Hardy greeted her
at the door. A man with a camera stepped behind
Jade and Mary Anna, both smiling so big for the
camera. This whole situation stunk so bad it could
knock a buzzard off a gut wagon.

"It seems like the whole town has gone crazy."
Hettie stopped me on the sidewalk in front of
Pose and Relax. She put the chalkboard sign with
the daily classes written on it on the sidewalk.

"Closed?" I questioned when I read the sign.

"Yeah." Hettie smiled. "Jade's assistant came
by and rented the entire store for the day. Jade
loves yoga and wants to film her sessions while
here."

"You've been Jaded," I warned. "Just like the rest of this town."

"What?" Hettie clasped her hands in front of her.

"First Higher Grounds, then Girl's Best Friend, now you," I growled. "Next thing you know, she'll try to get Granny to let her film the Inn and not to mention her plan for Jack."

"What about Jack Henry?" Hettie asked.

"Nothing." I shook off my gut feeling that Jade was somehow going to incorporate a lost love into her little TV show. After all, that would make her ratings soar.

"Don't tell me you won't be happy for Sleepy Hollow if we get a little publicity out of this?" Hettie made a good point.

"You aren't from here. I am." I pointed to myself. "Like my Granny said, pretty is as pretty does and she was not pretty."

"People can change and maybe this is her way of giving back." Hettie always did turn the glass half-empty theory into the glass half-full. "You've got everything you wanted." She went down the list. "You have Eternal Slumber all to yourself. Jack Henry is all yours. And you love living here."

"You're right." I took in a deep breath of fresh air. "Besides, we were kids. Of course people grow up, mature and change."

"Right. See." Hettie smiled. "Feel better?"

"A little." There was a knot in my gut. Most people change. Jade was not like most people.

I glanced down the street. The crowd had somewhat dispersed. It was a good time to walk down there and talk her into an exclusive with Fluggie.

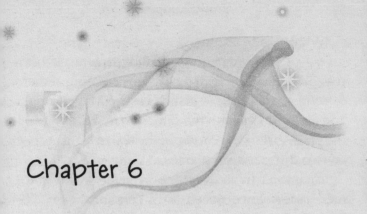

Chapter 6

L ook what the cat dragged in." Jade Lee, Tina Tittle and the young girl along with Marla and the camera crew were the only people in Girl's Best Friend Spa. "Or should I say the Grim Reaper?"

Jade giggled, pleased with her little funeral home dig. She was sitting in one of the stylist chairs with one of Girl's Best Friend black capes snapped around her neck. Mary Anna had on plastic gloves and used a paintbrush tool to brush on the goop of gel-like purple stuff on Jade's hair.

"Jade," Tina scolded her. Tina gave me a sympathetic look before she went back to flipping the pages of one of the many tabloid magazines Mary Anna had stacked for her clients to read while they got their hair done.

"What?" Jade shrugged. "I was just joking."

One of the cameramen positioned himself between me and Jade with the big lens pointing at me.

"Where are all the stylists?" I asked Mary Anna, and ignored Jade and the cameraman. I did notice the plain girl in the corner of the spa texting away on two different cell phones.

"I couldn't have everyone in here gawking at me." Jade's voice oozed with condescension. "I have to always buy up the shops for the day when I visit."

Mary Anna busied herself with the paintbrush to apply the color on Jade's exposed roots.

"But don't worry." Jade's upper lip curled up and she squished up her nose. "I won't be doing anything with Eternal Slumber while I'm here. I don't plan on using *your* services." She cackled.

"Oh no." Suddenly Mary Anna's happy-go-lucky attitude went straight down the tubes. She grabbed Jade by the arm and jerked her out of the chair.

Another cameraman flung a camera up on his shoulder and glued his eye to the viewer. He followed closely behind them.

"What?" Jade jerked away from Mary Anna's grip and turned to the camera. She straightened her shoulders, tilted her head to the side and chin down, giving the camera a nice big smile. She batted her lashes. The cameraman slid his eye from the viewer and looked at Jade with both of his eyes. A smile crossed his face. He looked through the viewer and circled the camera around Jade from all angles.

"This is the wrong color." Mary Anna pushed Jade down into the chair in front of the water bowl.

"Wrong color?" Jade asked. Her voice was uneasy with a spice of irritation.

Mary Anna pushed the chair back to a reclining position and turned the water on high pressure. She looked at me with a hint of weariness in her eyes. She worked her hands through Jade's hair as fast as she could as the water shot out of the sprayer at full speed and sloshed up against the sides of the bowl.

It was apparent that after five minutes of power washing Jade's hair and many different products Mary Anna had applied to the wet mess, the lime-green color was not going to wash out like Mary Anna had hoped.

"Give. Me. A. Mirror." Spit flung out of Jade's mouth with every word. "Now!" Her hand shot toward the young assistant.

The young girl gulped. In all my years of being an undertaker, I'd never seen the fear of death on anyone's face . . . until now.

The girl's hand was shaking as she lifted a handheld mirror up to Jade Lee's line of vision. "It is a nice shade of Jade," the girl squeaked.

"Jade!" Jade jerked the mirror down to her side. I swear, if her eyes could've thrown flames at her assistant, the girl would be charred right then and there. "You imbecile!" Her teeth clamped together; her lips moved at rapid speed. "If I wanted to wear the color of my name, don't you think I'd let a real professional do it and not this. . . ." Her eyes drew up and down poor Mary Anna, who was trembling in her stiletto heels. "This thing!"

Tina Tittle and I gawked in horror. Jade had completely lost her mind.

"Now, Jade," Mary Anna said in a sweet, angelic tone, "I can fix this."

Jade pushed herself up from the chair and moved the mirror back up to her face. Now, if it were me, I might have laughed and then started to cry, but clearly Jade was not me.

"You." Jade held her voice in a steady, low tone. She pulled the mirror down to her side. "You will never have another client as long as I'm living."

"But it was a simple mistake." Mary Anna talked fast, but Jade Lee was much quicker.

"Towel." She snapped her fingers at her assistant. The girl quickly got a towel.

"I'm sure this can be fixed," the girl squeaked. "And remember the reality deal."

At first Jade looked like she was going to wrap the towel around the girl's neck, but then she softened. She gripped the towel, twisting it around in her hands.

All of us sat there wondering what Jade was going to do with the towel. I kind of wanted her to twist it around and snap it at Mary Anna's legs like we did when we were kids at the swimming pool, but she didn't. She curled it around her head and made it into a turban.

"Mistake?" Anger seethed from every pore in Jade's body. She stalked toward Mary Anna. Mary Anna backed up until she was pressed against the rinsing bowl. She was stuck between porcelain and the devil. "Creamer in coffee is a mistake. This is an outrage and you are making me look bad. Out of the kindness of my heart I was going to give this so-called spa—which really is nothing more than five and dime—a little shout-out on my show, but I wouldn't send my dog here, much less my beloved viewing audience." Jade turned on the balls of her fancy shoes and took one step forward before she turned back around.

Mary Anna didn't move. It looked as though she'd become one with the bowl. She might've even dirtied her underpants. Now I'd for sure seen the fear of death on someone's face.

"I hope you have some other little skill you learned, because this"—Jade lifted her hand and snapped it in the air—"is over! I hope you got all that." She looked straight into the camera.

"Oh yes," the man agreed. "I got it."

The young assistant looked at Mary Anna and me with sad eyes before she took her place behind the cameraman who was behind Jade as they rushed down the sidewalk. Poor Tina Tittle lagged behind.

"I tried to warn people." I sighed, looking over at Mary Anna who was still in a state of shock. "I told you that you've been Jaded."

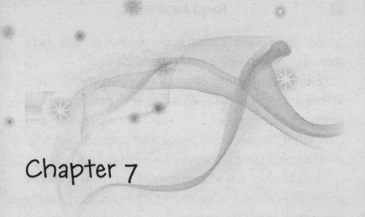

Chapter 7

It didn't take long for the scuttle between Miss Prissy Pants, aka Jade Lee Peel, and Mary Anna Hardy to spread throughout Sleepy Hollow, which made it a perfect time for me to approach Jade about doing that interview I had told Fluggie I'd set up.

The rocking chairs on the front porch of the Inn were taken by guests and not one of them was Jade, but one was the assistant. The white van I had seen earlier from where the cameramen had emerged was parked in the gravel parking lot next to the Inn.

"Hi there." I gave a slight wave on my way up the steps to the girl.

"Ms. Peel doesn't want any company." The girl's face was stern, her eyes forward.

"So." I shrugged. "I'm here to see my Granny. She owns the Inn." I pointed to the screen door. "I help out sometimes."

"Oh." The girl took her toe and rocked the chair back and forth at a less-than-soothing speed.

"You know." I sat down in the chair next to her when the other guest got up. "If you go at a slower pace, you will find your stress level will go down."

"There is no amount of rocking in this chair that will get rid of the tension in my shoulders." The girl let out a heavy sigh, giving another big push. "I mean." The girl looked at me as though she were pondering if she should talk to me. She continued, "It's hair."

"Green hair." I couldn't stop the smile as I spoke. I put my hand in the air and began to practice the pageant wave Marla Maria had taught me while I had my very brief stint as a pageant contestant when I was trying to help her husband, Chicken, cross over. *Elbow, wrist, elbow, wrist.* I did my best pageant wave and remembered how much I disliked all the beauty queen stuff. The things I did for my Betweener clients. "Can you imagine her riding around the town square in the morning with green hair?" A fit of laughter made me double over in my chair.

A cry of relief broke from her lips. "So I'm not being ridiculous?"

"Heck no." I covered my mouth with my hand to try to get the laughter to stop. Everything I have ever wished to happen to Jade when we were growing up had just come true. Just like Granny said, pretty is as pretty does and right now her pretty was only skin-deep.

"It was a little funny how her hair turned green like her name." Her shoulders shook as she tried to keep her laughter in. "It was fun while it lasted."

"Huh?" I asked.

"She went crazy on the phone with her stylist when we got back here from the spa and . . ." She pointed to her head. "She told the stylist she was fired if she didn't get here to fix her hair. She even had a private jet ready at the airport."

"Wow." I just couldn't believe the clout Jade had.

"I feel awful for how she treats people around here." The girl turned toward me. "Keisha Venford."

"Emma Lee Raines." I nodded back.

"Yeah. I know." Keisha's brows lifted. "Ms. Peel gave everyone the rundown of who we could talk to and film before we got here. And you are not on the list."

"No love lost." My insides burned. There was no way in hell I was going to ask her who was on the list and risk her telling Jade, giving Jade the satisfaction that I cared.

I did care. There were some choice words I wanted to call her other than her name, but that wasn't good Southern manners. Besides, I could bite my tongue for the next couple of days.

"She can be a bit of a pill." Keisha drummed her fingers on the arm of the chair. "She can be so nasty." Keisha's hand pulled up. She uncurled her finger and pointed it at me. "One of these days, she's going to cross the wrong person. Mark my words."

The screen door flew open.

"There you are!" Jade Lee screamed. Her face was covered in white cream, her hair pulled up in a scarf, and she wore a long, silk kimono. "You need to get ahold of that yoga teacher over there and cancel my appointment. I can't concentrate with this kind of hair."

"I'm sorry." Keisha jumped up. Trembling, she fiddled with her fingers. "I was getting some fresh air while you took a bath."

Keisha scurried into the Inn.

"You know," I said, stopping Jade when she turned to go back into the Inn. "You really need to do something about that temper."

"Temper?" Her brows cocked. "I don't have a temper. I just have very little tolerance for ignorance."

"The very people you are calling ignorant have supported you through this whole career you have going for yourself." I stood up. I had had it with her. "Mary Anna Hardy did nothing but change your hair color."

Jade cocked her head back, straightened her shoulders and her beady little eyes glared at me.

"You don't know anything," she spat out. She stepped back into the Inn. "If you have something to say to me, then you need to come inside. The world doesn't need to know my business."

I looked over my shoulder at the town square before I stepped inside and followed her into the room on the right where Granny kept the daily snacks. "Sleepy Hollow is no different now than it was when you lived here. Don't you know how you treated Mary Anna Hardy—someone who works and lives here, giving her life to this community—is already spreading in the gossip circles?"

I took a look at my fingernails to give her a little time to digest what I had said.

When I heard her suck in a deep breath and let out a long sigh, I went in for the kill.

"You know I'm right. No amount of movie star status will stop the real truth from turning into a bunch of gossip with a little extra added in." By extra, I meant how tales got twisted and turned into something completely different than how it started. "And more than hair gets twisted at a beauty shop, especially Girl's Best Friend."

"I'm guessing you have a better solution than my own publicist?" Her words held sarcasm, but I could tell she really wanted me to tell her my thoughts.

"I never said that." I smiled. "But I've lived here all my life and as an adult, I know how to smooth things over."

"Well, are you going to tell me or stand there like a lump on a log?" She planted her fisted hands on her hips.

I picked up one of Granny's famous oatmeal cookies and took a big bite out of it. Slowly I chewed, as Jade stewed in front of me.

"I really think you need to do an interview in the *Sleepy Hollow News*." I took another bite. "I mean it comes out tomorrow and you can kinda give your side of the story." I started to nod my head. "You know . . . the truth." My eyelids lowered.

Both of us knew the truth and she wasn't stupid. She knew exactly what I was saying.

"And I bet I can call in a favor to the paper." I sighed, brushing my hands together to get the crumbs off.

"You just might have something." She tapped

her chin with the pad of her pointer finger. "You know I can't look bad. The cameraman didn't shoot the best footage either."

"I'm sure." I was going to tell her whatever she wanted to hear to get Fluggie her interview. "So are you in or not?"

"What's in it for you?" Her head cocked to the side.

"You stay away from Jack Henry." It was as simple as that.

"You're kidding, right?" She laughed, throwing her head back. The scarf moved enough for me to see her hairline and a hint of green. "My audience is going to love the connection Jack and I share. A little JJ is going to make ratings soar." Her mouth dropped. Her eyes narrowed. "Wait." She smiled. "You and Jack?" She twirled around as if she'd just won the lottery. "Creepy funeral home girl and Jack Henry Ross?" She clasped her hands together in delight.

"Really? Are we still in high school?" I wasn't going to give in to her. I was holding the golden ticket with Fluggie Callahan in my pocket. "Deal or not? It's completely up to you."

If I could've smacked that grin off her face, I would have.

"Sure." She stuck her hand out for me to shake. I didn't bother.

"Your word is good enough." I pulled my phone out of my pocket and looked at the time. Jack Henry would be picking me up for dinner and then we were going to The Watering Hole for the prereunion party.

If I did my calculations right, Jade could have her interview with Fluggie while I was wooing Jack Henry at dinner, then she'd be at the bar when I walked in on Jack Henry's arm.

It was the perfect plan. I still needed to talk to Granny about the sideboard and her supposed wishes to be cremated, but there was no time. I was going to have to do a little magic of my own and get dressed up. If I was going to make my debut to our graduating class as Jack Henry Ross's girlfriend, I had to be as pretty as I could make myself.

I left the Inn, crossed through the square, stopping briefly at the gazebo where I took my phone out of my pocket and dialed Fluggie so I could give her the details and time of the interview. Needless to say, she was happy and my debt to her had been paid in full. More than full. If she only knew what it took for me to go to the Inn to specifically seek Jade out.

I also told Fluggie to make sure she followed Jade to the bar so she could get some shots of Jade having a good time with her buddies. Most importantly, I wanted Fluggie to get a photo of Jack Henry and me as we came in for the pictorial she was doing for the reunion weekend spread. That way, Jade Lee Peel would know good and well that JJ was long over and there was not a spark to be rekindled.

Chapter 8

"You are beautiful." Jack Henry's hand rubbed my bare thigh the entire way to Bella Vino Ristorante, our favorite restaurant. By his reaction, my decision to wear the black minidress was perfect.

"You make me feel beautiful." I put my hand on Jack Henry's. "And you don't think I'm the creepy funeral home girl anymore?"

"You are still totally the creepy funeral home girl," the familiar voice of Jade whispered in my ear. I jumped around and looked in the back of Jack's car. Empty.

"Did you say that I did look like creepy . . ." I started to ask Jack, turning back around in the seat.

"Are you kidding me?" His hand squeezed mine before he let go and turned the wheel right after we passed the small red-and-green sign that read *Bella Vino Restaurante*. "I never even thought you ever looked creepy in school. You were always so cute."

"Yeah, right," the voice snickered.

I cocked my head to the side to listen for more, but it was obviously my head messing with me. Jade Lee had me so worked up I was hearing her negative voice.

"I love you." Jack ran his hand down the back of my head and rested it on the back of my neck.

"I love you too." I smiled and let his hand rub away the tension that had settled there today.

The small red building was nestled in a wooded area. BELLA VINO was printed in white and outlined in green above the large windows that spanned the front of the restaurant.

"Why on earth would you even think I would even think you were creepy?" he asked. He turned off the ignition and turned in his seat toward me.

"That Jade Lee." I looked down at my hands even ashamed I had brought it up. "I told myself I was going to enjoy our dinner and not let her ruin it."

"Emma." He pushed my chin up with his finger. It took everything I had to look at him. When I did, it melted my heart.

"I saw you two this morning and high school flooded right back over me." I could feel the tears building up in my eyes. I blinked a couple of times to get them to go back down.

"That was ten years ago." He gestured between us. "This has more meaning and more substance than Jade and I ever had. I love you."

"But she told me that she was going to make it look like you two were rekindling things for ratings for her reality show." The sound of it made me sick.

"This is reality." He put his hand on the back of my neck and leaned in.

All things green, including Jade, melted away with the warmth of his lips and the deepening of his kiss.

"Let's skip dinner and the party and just go back to your place." His breath was hot on my ear. "That dress is driving me crazy." His lips trailed down my neck with a feathery touch and tantalizing persuasion before he gave me a few slow, shivery kisses.

"Good," I whispered. "The dress has done exactly what I wanted it to do. Keep your eyes on me all night."

I considered his proposal about going home, but wrenched myself out of his arms, leaving him wanting more.

"We have to go." I pulled the hem of the dress down on my thighs and tucked a piece of my hair behind my ear. "I'm the one hosting it for our class," I reminded him.

Technically, everything was done and the pre-event would go off without a hitch. There was no way I was not going to go and let Jade Lee Peel see with her own eyes that there was no longer a JJ. Jack Henry had picked me. End of story.

She might've given me her word at the Sleepy Hollow Inn to stay away from Jack Henry, but I didn't trust her one bit.

Jack Henry sucked in a deep breath. He rested the back of his head on the headrest and let out a long, steady sigh.

"If we have to." He tilted his eyes my way. "But you are all mine later tonight."

"I promise." I crossed my heart with my finger. "But I did hear that Mayor Burns asked her to join you as Grand Marshal of the parade."

I just couldn't let it go. No matter how much I tried, I couldn't.

"He did?" Jack Henry played it off. "I didn't know that. I guess we will see tomorrow morning."

That was what I loved about Jack. He was able to let things roll off his shoulders. If he could do it so could I.

He jumped out of the car, like he always did,

and ran around the front of the car to open my door. He put his hand out for me to take and helped me out.

"You are killing me." His eyes drew up and down my body. He gathered me into his arms and held me snug.

I wasn't going to lie. I did like how he looked at me. I enjoyed how his hands felt and I loved how he loved me.

The hostess took us into a private room where a table was set up for two. Jack pulled one of the two chairs out for me to sit down. The table was set with a red cloth. There was a chilled bottled of wine and two wineglasses on the edge of the table. The hostess poured a small amount and gave the glass to Jack. He swirled and twirled the wine in his glass as if he was some sort of wine expert. I knew better, but I enjoyed watching him play the game. He slung back the sip and nodded toward the hostess. She poured two glasses and took a step back.

"Enjoy your evening." The hostess blushed and stepped out of the room leaving us alone.

"Oh, I will love watching this fail," the voice responded to the hostess.

"What did you say?" I leaned over the table.

"I said here's to you," Jack picked up his glass. He tilted it a little to the side and held it up in the air for me to acknowledge his toast. "I'm proud of how you put this reunion together even though you weren't very fond of high school."

"Thank you." I picked up my glass and we clinked them together I couldn't help but look around. The only time I had heard voices was when I had Betweener clients. The voice was definitely Jade Lee Peel, but she wasn't dead.

I took another swig of my wine. I was letting her get to me. Like a big tidal wave, a line of chills grew up my legs, up my spine and across my arms.

"Are you okay?" Jack had the menu up to his face. He glanced over it. "You have goose bumps."

"I'm fine." I smiled. I was determined to have a good time and put Jade Lee in her place.

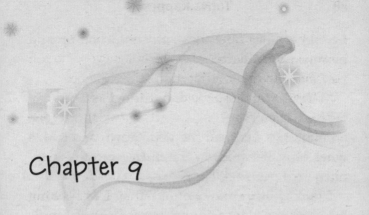

Chapter 9

My time alone with Jack Henry always went by way too fast.

The Watering Hole parking lot was packed when we pulled in. I was happy to see that Hoss had fixed the big boot sign and replaced the broken bulbs. It was the first time I'd seen it completely lit up in years.

The jukebox blared so loud, we could hear it from as far away as we had to park. Seeing Cheryl's car made my nerves calm, because the entire way here, Jack Henry told me about his day and I heard nothing. I was too busy trying to play out Jade's reaction when Jack Henry drew me near and professed his love for me in front of everyone.

I could see her face now—all scrunched up and glaring as I smiled and waved.

"Elbow, elbow, wrist, wrist," I whispered.

"What?" Jack asked, and turned off the car. "What did you say?"

"Nothing." I pulled the visor down and took a quick look at myself in the mirror before I reapplied my lipstick. "Ready?"

"Sure." Jack jumped out of the car and I got out before he made it around to get me. "Now, Emma Lee Raines," he scolded. "You know your granny would have my hide if she knew I didn't open your door."

"Lucky for you," I jabbed his rock-hard chest with my finger, "Granny isn't here, nor will she be at home tonight." I winked and did my best sexy sashay toward the bar.

"Uh-huh. I see ya." Jack ran past me, smacked his hand on my derriere and grabbed the door of the bar to let me in.

This was it. My big moment. The moment I've been waiting for for ten long years. The moment all of these people see me for who I am and not the creepy funeral home girl.

"Do you hear something?" Jack's hand had gripped the door handle. My breath was held, waiting for my big moment.

"No." I gestured for him to hurry and open the door.

From far away the wail of a siren stretched across to us. My heart sank. That sound meant that my night was probably not going to go as planned.

"I was so close," I muttered when a Sleepy Hollow patrol car came skidding into the parking lot and a deputy jumped out.

Jack Henry's instinct kicked in and he took off in the direction of the deputy like I'd seen him do so many times before.

They huddled together. The only thing I could hear was a low muffle.

"What's going on?" Fluggie Callahan asked when she opened the door of The Watering Hole. Her camera in hand, no doubt waiting for my arrival with Jack Henry for our societal debut in the *Sleepy Hollow News*.

"Lights! Police lights!" someone yelled from inside the bar. The jukebox went dead silent. Thunderous footsteps filled the space behind me.

Jack stepped back from the deputy. The siren had been turned off. The blue and white lights swirled around, lighting up the darkness surrounding us.

He held a clear bag in the air with something

red in it and brought it to his face to take a better look.

"My scarf!" Fluggie's voice escalated with excitement. "I lost it." She darted down the steps toward the cruiser. "Where on earth did you find it?"

The officer held it away from her when she went to grab it. The officer looked at Jack Henry; Jack Henry gave him the Baptist nod.

"This is your scarf?" Jack asked Fluggie.

"Yes, sir, it is." She grinned ear to ear and rocked back on her heels. "I made it with my own two hands."

"Fluggie Callahan, I need you to come down to the station." The deputy took a step back toward the door of his cruiser.

"Why in the world would you need me to do that? For a silly scarf?" Fluggie snarled.

"I need you to answer some questions about the murder of Jade Lee Peel." The deputy tucked his thumbs in the front of his pants.

"What? Murder?" she cried out, looking between Jack and the officer for some sort of clarification. When she came to the realization that she seemed to be a suspect, she blurted, "I didn't kill her!"

"We aren't saying you did." Jack had a way of not alarming people. His words were gentle. "But we did find this scarf around her neck and we are pretty sure she was strangled."

Fluggie put her hands on her head. "I swear I didn't kill her."

"That's fine, but we still have to ask you some questions." Jack gestured to the police cruiser. "Would you like to ride in the deputy's cruiser or drive down yourself?"

"I guess I'll drive down myself." Her voice was flat. She jerked her keys out of her pocket and stalked toward her car. She didn't look at any of our prying eyes.

"What is going on?" I asked Jack when he came back over to me. It wasn't like I didn't hear what had happened, but I sure wasn't grasping the fact that I had heard Jade Lee Peel was murdered.

He grabbed my hand and dragged me over to the side and out of people's earshot.

"Your granny found Jade Lee Peel dead with Fluggie's red scarf around her neck." Jack's words went in my ear, but they didn't register.

"Dead." I confirmed what I had heard for the second time. I shook my head as if there were cobwebs strung from ear to ear inside my head. "Wait." I shook even harder. "Around her neck as in stran—"

"Strangled." Jack Henry finished my sentence.

I turned around and everyone was staring at us. Even a couple of people were taking cell phone photos of us. This was definitely not how I saw Jack Henry Ross and I making the *Sleepy Hollow News* Societal page.

Chapter 10

The Sleepy Hollow Inn was crawling with police officers. Granny was in the kitchen hustling around and making coffee in the industrial pots she used for her Sunday brunches. Like everyone else, I was curious about what had happened and Granny was apparently the one to find our small town beauty queen dead.

Beulah Paige had her hand stuck down in a Higher Grounds Café to-go pastry box. She pulled out different petit fours, Danishes and scones, placing each of them on their own five-inch, white, French doilies. Then it was Hettie's turn to place them on silver serving trays. Poor old Mable Claire was eating every third one that Hettie put on the tray.

"Stop that." Hettie smacked Mable Claire's hand away. Mable pouted and scurried over to Granny.

"Tell me again." I encouraged Granny to tell me exactly what had happened just one more time. "Tell me exactly how you found her and who you called."

She smacked some dough in front of me on the counter and put the strap of an apron around my neck. I double wound the straps around my waist before tying it into a bow. I tucked my cell phone in the front apron.

"Roll. One inch." Granny pinched off some and had three homemade biscuits rolled and on the baking sheet before I even got one in the palm of my hand ready to roll. "If I told you once, Emma Lee, I told you a thousand times how I found Jade Lee Peel all laid out upstairs in the bathtub. Now, get to rolling."

"But I want to go over it one more time." I plopped the rolled-up dough on the baking sheet and pinched off more.

"Mable Claire." Granny grabbed the dough out of Mable's hands and pointed to the table. "You go on back over there and answer the phone if it rings."

Mable scowled but did as Granny said.

"This is the last time I'm telling you because we will have a bunch of people here and they will be expecting food. My food." Granny hurried over to the stove and turned down the boiling pot of water.

My mouth watered at the thought of her sweet tea. Granny was right. Whenever someone died, everyone gathered to discuss it over food. But a murder. That was an altogether different gathering. An all-night gathering of assumptions and gossip running wild.

"I had come home from Doc Clyde's because you know he's still trying to court me." She looked at me from under her brows and rolled her eyes. "What on earth does that man think? He's acting like we are teenagers." Granny nudged me with her elbow in my rib cage.

"Gross," I grunted. The last thing I wanted to hear were details about Granny's love life. Bless her heart—she'd already buried two husbands. If Doc Clyde was smart, he'd run. "Stop hemhawing around and tell me again."

"I was getting around to it and so not to get bored, I thought I'd start off this umpteenth time telling you by starting from the beginning of my evening." She unscrewed the sugar jar and took out the metal measuring cup filled with the tiny granules. "After Doc gave me a kiss to make my toes curls, I came in and did what I always do."

She held the measuring cup above the boiling

water and poured it in. The water sizzled. She filled the measuring cup a few more times and poured those in.

"Which is what?" My phone chirped from my pocket. I ignored it.

"I turned on all the lights because it's night and I check on all my guests." Granny's lip twitched.

"What are you leaving out?" I asked. I could tell she was leaving something out. "You were going to be nosy." My mouth dropped, my eyes narrowed. "You thought she was out at The Watering Hole for the preparty and you were going to her room to be nosy."

"Shh." Granny curled her head around; her eyes grew wide. "I was doing no such thing. And don't you go around accusing me of such."

"You were too," I whispered under my breath so no one else would hear.

"Well, it's a good thing I checked on her and found her." Granny spun her tale into a positive like she always did. "When they pack her out of here, you'll see she's still all pretty and not gray like most dead people."

"Granny," I scolded.

"It's the truth, ain't it?" She put her fingers in her short red hair and gave it a little fluff. "And all them cameras are out there waiting on her to come out."

"They are?" I had forgotten all about the cameras and the people behind them. I pinched another piece of dough and rolled it, pondering what they knew about Jade's death and why they hadn't been filming her.

Granny nodded her head and turned the gas stove off. The steam of the pot carried the sweet smell of tea throughout the kitchen.

"And you can't tell me you are mourning the loss. Not that you'd wish death on anyone, but you get my drift." Granny rolled a few more biscuits before placing the full baking sheet in the oven. She adjusted the knob.

"That is not fair." My phone chirped again. This time I took it out of the apron pocket and looked at it. It was a text from Jack Henry. "I have never wished death on anyone."

I untied the apron and took it off, hanging it on the hook next to the door leading out into the Inn so I could take a look at my text in private.

"So much for privacy." I sighed.

Just like Granny had said, the Inn was packed with members of the community who probably wanted to get a glimpse of Jade Lee's body as they carted her off to Eternal Slumber. Not that her father had asked me to host her funeral, but the county rented Eternal Slumber's morgue and the elected coroner, Vernon Baxter, worked for me.

Careful not to make eye contact, I slipped up the stairs to where the guest rooms were and down the hall. Jade Lee's room was full of officers that blocked the doorway. I rose up on my tiptoes when I passed, mainly out of curiosity. The entire room was silent.

Pastor Brown stood over the lifeless body, his head down, his eyes closed and his lips moving as he spoke a prayer over her. His hand was placed on Artie's back.

Poor Artie. My heart broke for the poor man. Jade was his only daughter and he sure was proud of her.

"Emma Lee." Vernon walked up behind me. He whispered, "Dang shame. So much life ahead of her. Did Artie say anything to you about having her as a client?"

"No." I shook my head. "I guess you drove the hearse over?"

"Yep. Here to pick her up." Vernon dipped his right shoulder and walked into the room. Everyone looked up at him. A feeling of sadness smothered the air.

They all had the look I'd seen so many times in my career. The look when the undertaker came to your door unannounced. An unwelcome sight.

My phone chirped again. I scurried down the hall.

I smiled when I looked at Jack's text name come across my phone.

Jack Henry: *Can you come down here? I have a few questions for you.*

Me: *About what?*

Why on earth would he have questions for me? While normally it took him a long time to text me back, now he was fast. I leaned my back on the wall between two guest doors.

Vernon walked out of Jade's room and I could hear his footsteps go back down the stairs. I knew what was coming next. Many times I had helped him with the church cart.

Jack Henry: *Come on down and bring me some of Zula's tea.*

Me: *See you soon.*

I hurried a text back because I needed to help Vernon.

I looked down at my dress. It was not proper attire to drag the heavy church cart up the stairs and I was definitely going to have to change my outfit before I went to the police station.

I pushed myself off the wall and began to walk back down the hall.

"I guess it's true?" Mary Anna Hardy stopped me in front of the guest room right after the stairs and just before Jade's room. "I came here to see for myself."

"The police cruisers and hearse out front didn't give you an affirmation?" I asked with a brow cocked, knowing Mary Anna had really come just to be nosy.

Both of us turned and looked to see what the loud sound clumping up the steps was. We stepped out of the way when John Howard Lloyd and Vernon climbed the last step and jerked the church cart, letting the wheels down. They barreled down the hall.

John Howard's hair was messy and wiry. He wore a pair of faded overalls and a red plaid shirt underneath. His black shoes had a little dirt ring around the thick soles. He'd been a full-time employee of mine for a few months now and he helped out wherever he could with odd jobs like cleaning, mowing, plucking leaves—everything that made the funeral home look nice.

"Why waste the taxpayers' dollars?" Mary Anna groaned and crossed her arms. "John Howard should just throw her over his shoulder and march her right on over to the morgue."

"Mary Anna," I scolded. "She was murdered and no one deserves that."

Even though I couldn't fully come to believe my own words because Jade had truly dug her own grave, I had to hide my dislike of her for the good of my job and my Southern manners.

"Emma Lee Raines, I don't know who you think you're kiddin'." Mary Anna's accent became heavy when she got sassy. "But you hated that woman long before my run-in with her this morning."

The guest door next to us jerked open. A woman with long black hair parted in the middle—who sort of reminded me of Morticia Addams from *The Addams Family* television show—stuck her head out the door. She made quick eye contact before slamming it shut.

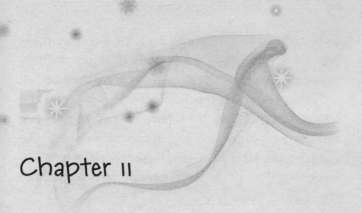

Chapter 11

"Granny," I busted through the swinging kitchen door. "When did the Addams family check in?"

I glanced around at all the Auxiliary women hustling around the kitchen. The smell of cinnamon, sugar and a touch of nutmeg made my stomach growl. Some people couldn't eat around death. Not me. I grew up around death and it was natural to me.

"Who?" Mable Claire jingled as she waddled over. She pulled a dime from her pocket and held it out between her finger and thumb. "Stop by and get you a piece of gum from Artie's."

"Thanks, Mable Claire." I didn't have the heart to not take it and offend her; she still thought me to be a little kid. Her jingle had good intentions behind it. She gave a piece of silver change to every child she'd pass as her day went along.

"I don't recall no one in Sleepy Hollow with the name Addams." Mable Claire bit her lip. I could tell she was digging back in her memory for the Addams family. In a small Southern town like Sleepy Hollow, your name meant more than your reputation.

No matter where you go in Sleepy Hollow, if someone doesn't recognize you, they will ask you your family name followed up by what you do for a living.

"Mable Claire," Granny fussed. "Emma Lee is making a joke about that girl with all that long hair and sullen eyes that's staying here."

"Now, now," Hettie Bell scolded, waving the doilies at us. "Y'all thought I was a Goth girl when I first came to town. Maybe she needs a friend." She went back to placing the doilies on the serving tray.

"You know"—Granny jumped around—"she did insist I relocate the guests in that room to a different room because she had to be next to Jade Lee. I don't make it a habit to find out every single thing about people who check into the Inn. That is illegal, you know."

"Hmm." I twisted my lips. I didn't recognize

her as part of Jade's crew and she was not someone Jade would've hung out with. My phone chirped. I glanced at it. It was Jack Henry wanting to know exactly how much longer I was going to be.

"Can I get a to-go cup for some tea? I'm going to take Jack Henry some."

"You tell him that he got the first glass of the batch." Cold air and a little cloud of condensation came out of the icebox when Granny opened it. She used the ice pick to get the perfect size cubes for Jack.

"I'm going home, changing my clothes and grabbing the car." I always told Granny my plans in case she ever needed me.

It wasn't like I had to. She could just pick up the phone and anyone could tell her where I was or they could find out. Someone was always watching.

She poured the warm tea into the glass. The ice crackled. Granny put a piece of plastic wrap over the mouth of the glass and sealed it. She handed it to me like a precious diamond.

"Perfect." I smiled and looked at the glass.

The ice wasn't to make the tea cold; it was to give the warm tea a shock and ignite the sugar granules. I always thought it was the best part of the tea process. Granny said it was in the glass. She never let anyone drink her tea out of a cup.

"Thank you." I bent over and kissed her.

"Now, don't you go packing tales about me snooping, ya hear?" Granny warned more than asked.

"Yeah, yeah. I got it." I walked toward the back door so I could avoid going through the Inn. "Granny, don't think all of this murder business gives you a pass on the sideboard Charlotte Rae wants and this nonsense about you being cremated."

Once I stepped outside, I glanced up the side of the Inn. The mystery girl was looking down from her guest bedroom window. She looked down. When our eyes met, the blinds slowly flipped closed.

Quickly I turned away and made a mental note to find out exactly who she was and why she had requested a room next to Jade's.

Her chilly stare made my hands shake the entire walk back across the town square to Eternal Slumber. Jack Henry was lucky because if it weren't for the plastic wrap Granny had sealed around the glass, there wouldn't have been any tea left when it got to Eternal Slumber, much less the police station.

The back entrance of the funeral home was the residence entrance into my little apartment. Before Charlotte Rae and I took over, there had been an entire family unit where we grew up. But we knew we had to remodel and upgrade. I only wish I'd done the sound system now that I'd been to Hardgrove's Legacy Center.

The door opened up into a small hallway with a little table and mirror. The room on the right was my bedroom and the room on the left was a little television sitting room with a couch. There was a communal room in the funeral home with a microwave and refrigerator if I need to heat up something or store perishables, but mostly I ate with Granny at the Inn or out with Jack Henry.

It was a great place to live and it was perfect for me.

I flipped on the light switch inside the door and stepped in. I put the glass of tea on the little table and glanced at myself in the mirror and looked at all the makeup I had applied. More than usual, but all the fashion magazines I'd read in line at Artie's Meat and Deli stated that you need to apply heavy makeup in photos and I had really planned on Fluggie snapping that photo.

"Just one more thing you ruined," I whispered thinking about Jade Lee.

I pulled the dress over my head and headed into the bedroom. I took my jeans and sweatshirt off the dresser and slipped them on. Comfort. A happy sigh escaped me. It would take too much time to wash all of the gunk off my face, so I swiped my lips with some cherry-flavored lip gloss and took one last look in the hallway mirror.

"If he was mine, I'd always be dressed to the nines so he'd always go gaga." The familiar voice was hidden in the darkness of the television room. "Or I'd slip on a little lacy number to jog his memory on how much he loves being a boy."

I peeked in to see if I had accidentally left the television on or if Jack Henry had. It wasn't unusual for Jack Henry to stop by when he had a free moment to relax and watch TV, even when I wasn't home.

"Seriously, you looked so good in that dress. You should probably put on a tighter shirt or something." Jade Lee glowed in the darkness. There was a sparkling tiara like a cake topper on her head. "Your Walmart bra kinda makes me sad."

I gulped.

"Wait." Her jaw dropped; she slid a little closer leaving a little path of glitter behind her. She came into the light. Wisps of blond hair stuck out from underneath a pink turban that matched a long silk kimono loosely tied around her waist. She wore a pair of heels with a pink pom-pom on the open toe. The tiara glistened on top of the turban. "You can see me, can't you?"

Ahem, I cleared my throat and pretended not to see her.

No, no, no, the voice in my head begged. *Anyone but her,* the little voice kept talking to me. *Anyone but her. Anyone.*

The sound of some rattling around in the basement of the funeral home meant that Vernon was here, Jade's body was in the basement and the hearse was back in the driveway.

I picked up the glass of tea and grabbed the hearse keys off the table and walked out of the funeral home slamming the door behind me.

"Oh my God," I whispered, my feet carrying me a mile a minute. I had to get out of there. "Oh God," I said it again. "I knew I had heard her talking to me earlier on my way to the restaurant, but noooooooo." My lips formed an O as I dragged out the word no. "I thought I was hearing things."

I got into the hearse and slammed the door. I looked in the rearview mirror and no Jade-ghost was there. I looked out the windshield and my window. Relief settled in my heart when I didn't see her.

"Thank you, Lord." I let out a deep sigh, put the glass of tea in the cup holder and turned the ignition.

"That's exactly what I told the big guy when this here tiara was waiting for me when they were trying to get me to walk down the golden pageant aisle in the Great Beyond." Jade Lee sat next to me in the passenger side and gently touched the tiara. She stuck her hands up in the air. "Thank you, Lord!" she screamed and nodded her head. "I said it just like that. Thank you, Lord!" she repeated.

"I got it the first time," I groaned, and planted my head on the steering wheel.

"Well." Jade Lee turned in the seat toward me. "I'll be a yellow-bellied sapsucker, you can see me, hear me and help me."

"Yes." I sat up and looked at her. "I can see you. I can hear you. But help you? Never."

"Creepy . . . um . . . Emma Lee." She flashed her pretty pageant smile. "We go back a long way. You wouldn't do a friend this way would you?"

"A friend I would help. You, not so much." Suddenly my mouth dried up. The tea looked awfully wet and appetizing. I picked up the glass and ripped off the plastic.

"Don't you dare." Out of nowhere, Jade's hand came flying across the seat and the glass flew out of my hands into the back of the hearse. "Do you know how many calories are in Zula Fae's sweet tea? My daddy always said he'd stay in business as long as Zula Fae came in and bought all those bags of sugar. And if you stole my sweet Jack Henry from me, then you need to count your calories and dress a little better. Oh!" She stuck her finger up in the air. "You need to get rid of those granny panties. If you can't find some acceptable thongs around here, then just don't wear any."

"What are you? The fashion police of the ever after?" I spat, a little embarrassed she, of all people, knew about my undergarments. It was hard enough for me to dress myself for Jack Henry, but downright disgraceful for my number one enemy to be giving me advice from the Great Beyond.

"You are talking to me," Jade singsonged to me.

"Okay." I gripped the wheel. My knuckles turned white and my fingers tingled as they started to go numb. "Let's get one thing straight. I have no respect for you. I tried so many times to be your friend in high school and all you did was call me Creepy Funeral Home Girl." My eyes lowered. "Do you know how much that hurt me? Do you?"

She drew back. Suddenly she didn't look so big and bad. More like weak and wilted, so I took the opportunity.

"As for Jack"—I pointed at her—"he is mine. Fair and square. He tells me he loves me. He tells me I'm pretty the way I am and we have sex!"

The peck on the window made me jump out of my skin.

"Emma Lee," Doc Clyde asked through the glass. "Are you okay?"

I waved my hand at him. There was no way I was rolling down the window. The damage had been done. He'd seen me talking to Jade Lee, which made it look like I was talking to myself and as sure as I was sitting in this hearse, he was going to run and tell Granny no matter what I said.

"I'm fine." I put the hearse in gear and peeled out of the driveway.

Chapter 12

So I was right." Jade looked even prettier in death. It made me sick. "You are the creepy funeral home girl who can see dead people. Kinda cool, especially now that you seem to be my new best friend."

"No and no." I wagged my finger at her and continued to drive to the police station. "I'm the only one that can help you get to the other side. I'm not in the market for a new best friend. Especially you."

Just like Jade Lee Peel, she ignored my comment about not wanting her to be my best friend. She never took no for an answer, which was probably how she got to be so popular, yet so disliked.

"Why would I want to go to the other side?" she asked. "I've got this great tiara and they didn't force me to walk down the gold walkway. Though it was tempting because I love anything gold." Her voice rose an octave.

"Don't you want your dad to have some sort of closure or bring your murderer to justice?" I slammed on the brakes after I had a sudden realization. "Fluggie Callahan didn't kill you."

"Kill me? Murder?" Her face squished up. "The newspaper lady?"

"If you are still here, then your murderer is still at large." I pushed on the gas. I couldn't wait to get to Jack Henry and get Fluggie out of jail. "And someone used Fluggie's scarf to kill you."

That was how this Betweener gig worked. My client wasn't able to cross over until their murder was solved and their killer was in police custody. If Fluggie Callahan was Jade's killer, Jade wouldn't be here with me.

Good thing for Fluggie. Bad thing for me. I had a feeling I was going to be spending a lot of time with Jade. Jack Henry was the only living person who knew about my secret, which meant I was going to have to tell him about Jade's ghost.

My stomach churned. I felt sick and a little light-headed. Jack Henry and I worked closely on solving a Betweener client's murder with the ghost, which meant Jade Lee was going to be a third-wheel in my relationship.

My heart pounded. The sudden burst of urgency to solve her murder was now more important than ever. We were going to have to mend fences and I could see I was going to have to talk her into crossing over once we did find her killer.

"Whoa!" Jade put her hands up in the air. Her fingernails were painted with sparkly polish and twinkled like the tiara on her head. "I was murdered? As in someone actually wanted to kill me? Me?" She planted her hand on her chest and arranged the look of disbelief on her face.

"Sun don't shine on the same dog's tail all the time." I knew it was an awful thing to say and that I should've felt bad she was dead, but I still said it.

"Well, I never." She pulled back, her jaw dropped. "I didn't deserve to die and that was an awful thing to say, even if you did say it in those silly terms."

"And you have to go to the other side. End of story!" I smacked the steering wheel.

I glanced over and she was gone.

"Good." I huffed. There was no way I was going to let her ghost linger around. I was on a mission. I had to find her killer and get them behind bars. My relationship with Jack depended on it.

Media vans and the white van I had seen Jade's personal camera crew emerge from had taken up the few parking spaces at the police station.

"My goodness." Jade reappeared. "All of this for little ole me?" Her Southern accent dripped with charm. Fake charm. "How do I look?"

"Dead."

"Oh, go on." She smiled and touched the tiara. "How do I look, Emma Lee?"

"It doesn't matter. They can't see you." I reminded her she was a ghost.

Her smile faded. Her face drooped. Her chin dropped.

"What about all those ghost photos with orbs and stuff?" She asked a good question. Her eyes twinkled, her teeth sparkled. "I mean, my tiara is so bright and beautiful, I bet I'm a glowing, marvelous orb."

I let out a long sigh and shut off the hearse. She'd already ghosted herself out of the car and paraded in front of the cameras like she was on a runway. The cameras were rolling and flashes were clicking, only they were on me and the hearse.

With my head down, I hurried into the Sleepy Hollow Police Station. Questions hurled at me. I felt like I was dodging bullets. Once I was safe inside the door, I glanced back to see what the beauty queen was doing.

I shook my head. Her face was stuck inside one of the lenses of the camera and she waved and talked like they could see and hear her.

"Bless her heart," I whispered, feeling a little sorry that she felt her worth was only in the eyes of a camera.

"Bless whose heart?" Familiar arms curled around my waist and pulled me close. The sweet voice of Jack Henry Ross sent chills down my body.

"No one." I turned around and gave him a nice hug in return since everyone in the station was looking at us, including Fluggie Callahan, who was gripping the bars of the jail cell.

"Where's my tea?" Jack asked.

"Oh. That." I groaned. I was going to have to tell him sooner or later. Sooner was best because I had no intention of being in a relationship with Jack and a lusty ghost who used to date him as our third wheel. "We need to talk."

I grabbed his hand and dragged him to the corner of the station.

"'You aren't going to believe who didn't register as a contestant for the big pageant in the sky." I pinched my lips and held my breath.

"No." Jack's eyes popped open.

Slowly I nodded my head up and down. Nervously he ran his hands through his hair while he looked around to see if anyone had been staring at us. Of course they were. All of their eyes were trained on us.

"I'll be right back," Jack said to the deputy and grabbed my hand.

He dragged me into the storage closet and shut the door behind us.

"Are y'all neckin'?" Jade Lee appeared and asked in a twang. She pursed her lips and made kissy noises.

"No we are not," I said, and sucked in a deep breath.

"Jade?" Jack Henry asked.

"He knows you can see me?" A big smile crossed her lips as she curled up to him. She pushed her hair over her shoulders and took a long whiff of his hair. "Yummy. He always smelled so good."

"Stop it right now," I said through gritted teeth.

"What is she doing?" Jack glanced around the small space.

"Nothing." I shook my head. I wasn't about to give her the satisfaction of telling Jack Henry her crazy antics.

"Tell him that I love him in death too." She winked. Her finger dragged across his shoulder.

"We have to solve her murder. Now." I stomped. I could feel all the blood in my body rush to my face.

"She really has you flustered." A wry smile caught his lips. "And you are so cute flustered."

"Forget any of that." I waved my hand in front of me. "There is no way her ghost is going to let us have our time alone. Just so you know."

"Which means we need to start working on her murder." Jack was talking my language.

"Exactly." I snapped my fingers and pointed at him.

Jade Lee brought her hand up in front of her face and put her fingers together. "You know, I've never been able to snap." Her hand bobbled up and down as she tried, her wrist loose.

"I'll teach you later. Right now you need to focus." I turned to her.

"Focus. Got it." She gave the aye-aye-captain salute. "Focus on what?"

"Jack is going to ask you some questions." I nodded toward Jack.

"Tell me about your entire day from the time you showed up in Sleepy Hollow until your last recollection before you were . . . um . . . murdered."

"He is so cute. He always did that little lip thing when he didn't want to hurt my feelings." Her shoulders curled up around her ears, her nose squished.

"You've never done the lip thing for me when you hurt my feelings." I pointed to his mouth.

"What lip thing?" The line between his brows creased.

"Nothing." I shrugged it off. Why on earth was I fussing with a ghost when he, the real living and breathing man, was standing in front of me.

"Aw. He's so cute." Her voice rose an octave. "Here is a perfect example of how you could use my advice." She huffed. She twirled around the small space we were standing in. "This is a perfect place to get in some good smooching time. It might seem childish, but men never leave their childish ways behind. They love spontaneity."

"We can't focus on spontaneity when you are dead and your murderer is out there." I asked, "What happened to focus?"

"Focus. Right." She pulled her hand up and tried to snap again. She looked disappointed, and said, "I got into town and saw you right off."

"No you didn't," I corrected her.

"What? What did she say?" Jack asked.

I held a finger up.

"You didn't see Jack Henry first," I corrected her again. "You got into a fight with a person in a car because they were parking too close to your car."

"Oh." She blushed. "You saw that?"

"Not only did I see it, but I heard you clear across the town square while I was doing yoga class with the Auxiliary women in the gazebo."

I rolled my eyes. She had no idea how bad she treated people and she had no clue that people knew she treated others badly.

"Then you saw Jack and Beulah Paige had rushed over before the film crew got out of the van." That was where she wanted to start the story.

"Yes." She had totally erased the incident with the car out of her mind.

"What did the car look like?" Jack Henry asked.

"Red." She smiled.

"No it was not red. It was green." Frustrated, I sucked in a deep breath and slowly let it out, mentally saying Granny's motto. *Breathe in Jesus, breathe out peace.* I repeated it again. "I'm sure you can get the video footage from the courthouse to see the argument."

"The driver could have motive." Jack's brows lifted.

"Yep. Angry. Embarrassed. And she had no qualms about her to even think she was wrong." I watched as Jack jotted things down in the notepad he'd pulled from his jacket pocket.

"And don't forget about Beulah Paige. She never forgets a thing. Especially something someone big and famous would do and say."

Beulah Paige Bellefry was the CEO and gossip queen of Sleepy Hollow. No matter if it was all true or even a tiny flea bite true, she told it.

Jack wrote as fast as I could translate what my new Betweener client told me about her day. She told us about her spa experience and failure with Mary Anna up until her interview with Fluggie Callahan.

"Don't forget about Keisha. Did you have any ill words with her?" I asked.

She shook her head side to side.

"Are you sure?" I asked, knowing deep down what Keisha thought about her. Not that I thought Keisha was the one to off Jade Lee, but no stone unturned had been the key to my Betweener job. Every lead was important, no matter how small or big and Keisha might have seen something or heard something.

And I felt it strange I hadn't seen Keisha since Jade was found dead.

"Where is Keisha?" I asked Jack Henry.

"I have no idea who this person is." Jack shrugged.

"She is Jade's assistant." I gave him a quick description and he vaguely remembered her. "What about Morticia Addams?" I couldn't erase her from my mind if I had tried.

"As in the TV show?" Jack Henry asked. I was confusing him more than helping him.

I turned to Jade. "Who is the lady with all the black?"

"Patricia?" Jade cackled. She threw her head back and her tiara teetered. She quickly straightened it back up. "Morticia. You sure are a funny one. Who knew?" She shrugged, her hands in the air. "Patricia is my stylist. I forced her to come in to fix my hair that Mary Anna ruined."

I told Jack the story about Patricia and who she was. No wonder she insisted that she have a room next to Jade. It was perfectly normal in Jade's circle to request things.

"Tell Emma everything you remember up to waking as a ghost," Jack Henry said into the air next to me.

"She's right there." I pointed next to him. "She's kinda got a thing for you still."

"Emma." She gasped like I had completely embarrassed her. "I swear I have no idea how you captured Jack Henry Ross's heart. I mean, you could use a little lipstick. It adds color to your face and you look like you could use all the color you can stand."

"Can you please answer his questions so we can get this whole murder thing figured out?" I asked. It was one thing to get advice from a living beauty queen, but from a dead one? No thank you.

She put her finger in a loose wisp of hair that stuck out of the turban and twirled it around. Then she tapped her chin. She let out a little moan and a sigh. "Hmm." Her lips puckered to the side. "Well, I had that interview with the *Sleepy Hollow News*."

"And," I encouraged her to continue.

"Patricia fixed my hair and I paid her a lot of money to do so." She continued to play with the edges of her hair. "Then." She stopped, her face contorted. "That's it."

"That's it?" I questioned her. She nodded. "Are you sure? Because nothing seems out of sorts. You had a fight with Mary Anna and Marla Maria."

"Marla Maria?" Jack asked.

"I forgot about Marla Maria," I snapped. "She was madder than Lady Cluckington when she gets a bath."

"She wanted me to do free service announcements for her pageant school." Jade rolled her eyes. "For free!"

I filled Jack Henry in on all the facts and what I had seen earlier in the day.

"Not that I think Marla killed Jade, but weirder things have happened." I pinched my lips together.

"I need to interview Beulah, Mary Anna, Zula Fae, Keisha and Patricia to start with." Jack read down the list of names he'd made while Jade told her day's events. "I also need to add Marla Maria to the list."

"I'll help," I said.

"No you won't," Jack said.

This was always the part during my Betweener gig where he said he had to take over because it was the police's job and he had to be careful with the information the ghosts gave him or else people would think he was nuts like me. And they would question where he'd gotten his insider information.

"Leave it to the police." He had to put that sweet spin on it. "What on earth would I do if you got in the cross fire?"

"Aww." Jade smiled.

"It's not like Beulah or anyone on your list is a hardened criminal—that we know of—and if I see them at an event or the café, I can slip in questions if it allows." It sounded good, but that was not my intention. I was totally planning on making a conscious visit to each of them if time allowed.

"Only and only if you happen to have the right opportunity." Jack's voice held an unspoken warning.

"What about the scarf?" he asked.

"She left it there after the interview." Even her ghost had a smug look. "What?" I must've made a nasty face at her because she was looking directly at me.

"And you just remember her leaving and that

is where your memory ends?" Jack asked. She nodded. I told him her gesture. "You have no idea who killed you or wanted you dead?"

"No. I know it was someone who was jealous of me," she spat. "Emma Lee, where were you when I was murdered?"

"You've got to be kidding." I swear I wanted to punch her in her perfect face.

"What?" Jack Henry asked.

"She thinks I'm jealous of her. I swear if I didn't think she'd bother me and you, I'd refuse to help her one little bit to cross over."

"That just isn't nice." Jade had curled back up around Jack, making me fume.

There was a light rap on the door.

"I hate to disturb your ten minutes in the closet, but the press is practically beating down the doors of the station," the deputy said.

I glared at the ghost of my archnemesis.

"We have to get her crossed over." My words were sharp. "If not, she's going to be like a bugger I can't thump off."

I had a feeling if I didn't get her crossed over as soon as possible, I might be Jaded.

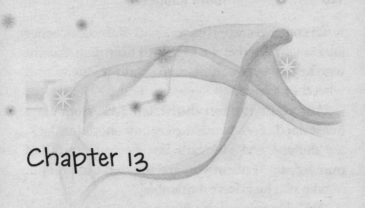

Chapter 13

"Psst, Emma Lee." Fluggie waved me over. Her hand flailed between the cell bars. "You've got to get me out of here. Show that boyfriend of yours some skin or give him a little somethin', somethin' if you know what I mean. You really owe me now."

"How do I owe you? I got you that interview. It's not my fault you left your scarf there." I looked over my shoulder to see what all the rigmarole was about.

Jack Henry and the deputy were hunkered over his desk in deep discussion. The deputy looked at me, and then back to Jack Henry.

"How did you know that?" Fluggie snapped back. "I didn't tell anyone about the scarf and my lawyer has yet to show up."

Oh crap. Oh crap. This was part of the Betweener job I wasn't good at. I had a hard time distinguishing the line between the living and the dead and what they told me.

"Are you sure you didn't tell Jack Henry?" I questioned, and pointed over my shoulder. Jack, the deputy and Fluggie's lawyer were huddled over a desk. "I mean you are stressed out and all. Maybe you just don't remember."

"No." Fluggie wasn't buying it. "I'm a reporter and I know what I did and didn't say. Do you think this is stressful? Heck no. I've been in so many jails over protesting that this is almost a second home." She grabbed my shirt through the bars and curled her fist deep in the cotton pulling me closer. "I've got to get out of here so I can kick whoever's ass needs to be kicked for making it look like I killed that girl."

"Take it easy." I smacked her hand away from my sweatshirt and ran my hand over the wrinkled-up cloth to straighten it back out.

"Tell me how you knew about the scarf." The tone in her voice told me she wasn't kidding. After the deputy had questioned some of the Inn guests who put Fluggie at the scene of the crime at the approximated time of death determined by Vernon Baxter, he read her Miranda rights to her, and then she lawyered up.

"Duh." Jade appeared on the little cot in the cell. She bounced up and down. "These things are uncomfortable. Oh." Jade lifted her hand and did her best to snap those fingers, but failed. "Tell her that I called you and told you about the scarf."

"Or maybe Jade told me that you left your scarf and she was going to give it to me to give you." If Jade Lee thought I was going to be any nicer to her for helping me out, she was wrong.

"Emma Lee, being too honest was always your problem in high school." She continued to bounce up and down. "That's why we never invited you to go to the caves for parties or anything. We knew you'd tell and that nosy granny of yours would've told our parents."

Fluggie looked over her shoulder as though she was trying to see what I was looking at.

"It's called being a good girl." The voice escaped my mouth before I could shut it. "I mean . . ." I gulped and looked at Fluggie. "She called to thank me for setting up the interview and then she mentioned the scarf."

"Oh." Fluggie's eyes darted between my eyes. She was trying to read me and I tried to have the best poker face, but Jade was right. I wasn't good at lying or keeping things swept under the rug.

"Excuse me." The deputy came over and unlocked the cell. "Your lawyer made bail for you.

Don't leave town." He opened the bars. "Sheriff Ross is outside addressing the media. You can go out the back door and avoid them. There is a deputy out there to take you back to your car."

Fluggie didn't wait a minute longer. She darted out of the cell and pointed her finger at me.

"You. Me. Old mill, nine a.m." She stomped out of the station. "Don't be late."

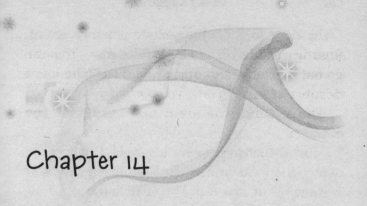

Chapter 14

I tossed and turned all night long. Mainly waiting to see if Jack Henry was going to stop by or if Jade Lee was going to show up. Neither happened.

Jack was occupied with chasing leads that probably led to nowhere. This was how he did things. Several leads would come in from people who thought they saw something and he would run off to investigate. It was good for me because I would only take what my Betweener clients told me and go on the down-low to investigate myself.

There was no way I wanted Jack to know I took matters into my own hands, and if anyone in the community saw me talking to Jade, it would look like I was crazy.

The door lock on the private entrance to my apartment rattled. Excitement filled me with hope it was Jack Henry coming to rest after a long night of investigating.

"Emma Lee?" Granny's voice came from the door.

I pulled the covers over my head. I had yet to change the locks and when Granny felt the need to come on in, she did. Fortunately for all of us, she'd yet to feel the need when Jack Henry stayed over.

"Are you still in the bed?" Granny turned the corner into my bedroom. She flipped on the light. "Get up. It's six o'clock and it's not good for your mental health to sleep all day."

I peeked out of the top of my covers and threw them back. Surely to God my eyes were deceiving me. I picked the crusty sleepies from the corners of my eyes, sure they were clouding my vision. I blinked a few times, but the sight still didn't go away. Granny had on a gold sequin floor-length gown that matched her red hair and skin tone perfectly.

"I don't have to be at the square until seven." I reminded her about the time the participants were going to gather before the parade. "You sure are all gussied up to be only serving tea all day."

I got out of bed and walked over to her. She

hadn't been this dressed up since her wedding day to Earl Way Payne.

Granny always made her famous sweet tea for events held in Sleepy Hollow and she always had a big line.

"Oh no." Granny shook her bony finger. She batted her eyes. The long black fake eyelashes were curled to high heaven.

"Do you have on fake lashes?" I walked over and held my finger out to get a feel. "Did Marla Maria get her claws into you?"

"Stop that." Granny smacked my hand away. "I've been working on these babies for an hour." She proudly batted them again. "O'Dell Burns made sure there was no parade."

"What?" Shock waved over me. The last thing I had thought about was the parade being canceled.

"He said it wouldn't look good if we had it. Something about cameras and national attention." She shrugged. "I guess all them camera vans out there should tell you something. Come to think about it, I think I saw that person from the *Today Show* out there."

"Where?" I slipped off my pj's and threw on a pair of jeans and a shirt and pulled my hair back in a ponytail.

"All over." Granny fussed with a stray hair hanging down in her face.

"So you are gussied up for the cameras?" My eyes narrowed. I knew there was something behind her madness.

"Listen, if Jade Lee Peel could get a reality show, surely to God we can get one." She rambled. "I mean I run the Inn, you run the funeral home, plus the town thinks you're crazy and now that your 'Funeral Trauma' is acting up . . ."

"You wait right there," I interrupted her.

"Emma Lee, Doc Clyde told me he saw you just having the best conversation in your hearse with no one." Granny's perfectly drawn-on brows lifted. "Between me and you and all the gossip around here, we're sure to entertain some people. And if the film crew is already here, I figured I'd pitch them my idea."

"Oh, Granny." I took one quick look in the mirror before I headed to the bathroom to brush my teeth. Granny continued to spout on about her crazy idea of a reality show. I wasn't sold on it. Look where it got Jade. Dead. "You've been Jaded."

Reality show? I looked at myself in the bathroom mirror and pondered on the reality show aspect of Jade's life. It was definitely something to explore. Did she have a viewer who was obsessed with her like the rest of Sleepy Hollow seemed to be? Did she make someone on the crew mad?

These were the questions I asked myself with my Betweener clients while Jack Henry followed up on what he called solid leads. Well, one thing was for sure, someone killed Jade Lee Peel and tried to frame Fluggie Callahan for it.

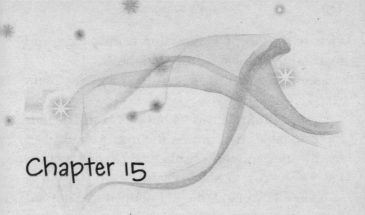

Chapter 15

After I rushed Granny out of my apartment, I grabbed my cell off the charger and decided to go ahead and get my day started. That meant walking down to Higher Grounds Café to get my jolt of caffeine.

Granny had caught me so off guard, I had completely forgotten to ask her about the sideboard and the silly notion she wanted to be cremated. Probably another one of Charlotte Rae's hare-brained ideas.

Network camera vans from all over were parked bumper to bumper, clear around the curb of the town square. Each of them had large steel antennas bolted on top. Most of the reporters were standing in the grass of the square with a view of the Sleepy Hollow Inn behind them and their cameraperson focused on them.

I slipped down the sidewalk and across Main Street.

Higher Grounds was as busy as ever. The four top café tables that dotted the inside were taken up by most of the regulars, including Beulah Paige Bellefry and Mable Claire.

"Good morning, ladies." I nodded and noticed there were three cups of coffee and only two people. "Can I sit down?"

I had plenty of questions to ask Beulah, but now wasn't the time.

"No." Beulah was not a fan of me. "That seat is taken. Don't you see the coffee cup there?" She jerked the empty chair up closer to the table, clearly not welcoming me to sit there.

"Oh my stars." I put my hand up to my chest. "I figured you were double fisting to get the grumpy away, but I guess not."

"I swear, Emma Lee, you are crazier than Doc Clyde says you are." Beulah twisted her head to look away from me and lifted her chin.

"Mable Claire." I smiled and walked on past up to the counter where Cheryl Lynne was filling the pastry case with fresh muffins and scones.

"Nothing like a murder to get business going."

Cheryl joked about the full café. "What'll ya have?"

"Large coffee." My eyes wandered over the contents of the glass case. I pointed to the apple scone. "Two of those."

While Cheryl scurried behind the counter to fill my order, I took my phone out of my pocket and thumbed through my contacts until I got to Fluggie's name. I quickly texted her to see if she was already at the old mill so I could stop by.

There was no reason to hang around town, in the mess of the camera trucks, if I could start working for my Betweener client. Which made me wonder where exactly Jade had run off to?

Fluggie responded back with: *Hell yes. Get over here.*

"Can you make it two large black coffees?" I asked when Cheryl slid the glass case door open to get out the scones.

"Not two creamers?" she asked. "Because I know Jack likes two creams."

"Just black," I confirmed and looked away when her eyes assessed me.

"Any news on Jade?" Cheryl asked.

"No, nothing." I shook my head. "Jack must be really investigating because I haven't seen him since last night when I went to check on Fluggie."

"How is she?" Cheryl wiped down the counter.

"She claims she's innocent and she accidently left her scarf at Jade's after she interviewed her." I shrugged.

"That's too bad." Cheryl looked at the door when the bell dinged announcing more customers coming in. "Business is booming. The entire world is watching."

Great, I inwardly groaned hoping the entire world didn't notice my little conversations with my Betweener client. Cameras were everywhere. I had to be extra careful.

After I paid and had my goodies in my hand, I turned back around and found out who occupied the third seat at the coveted table. Tina Tittle.

"Tina." I nodded. "I guess you'll be going home now that the parade and apparently the reunion is canceled?"

"You'd guess wrong." Tina picked up the cup and took a sip. "I wanted to stop by Artie's and see what I could do for him. I just feel awful for him."

"It is awful." I sucked in a deep breath and glanced around, surprised Jade hadn't showed up yet.

"You are such a good girl." Beulah patted Tina's hand and slid her eyes up to me. "You could take a lesson or two, Emma Lee."

"Nah." I curled my nose. "Enjoy your visit."

I hurried back down to the funeral home and grabbed my keys. I could hear Vernon Baxter in the basement. I was sure he was busy on the autopsy and collecting all the data he needed to get Jack some answers about Jade's body.

I resisted going down. I would let him get a little more done and maybe stop by later in the afternoon when he might have some more answers. Not that he'd tell me.

When I put the hearse in reverse, I noticed a few of the reporters running across the street to the funeral home with their cameramen on their heels.

"We understand Jade Peel is in there undergoing an autopsy." One reporter shouted through the window. Her microphone struck against the glass. "Can you tell us what they might be looking for?"

I held my hand up against the window to shield any sort of video they were taking of me and threw the hearse in gear, zooming out of town as fast as I could.

Of course I had to slow down at all the country road's curves, but I kept my eye out for anyone following me. I'd seen those cop shows where news crews followed people to get an angle on a story.

The old mill had recently been rebuilt and Fluggie rented it for the *Sleepy Hollow News* offices from Leotta Hardy, Mary Anna's mamma. Unfortunately, Fluggie was the only employee at the time, but she was well on her way to becoming bigger.

"Knock, knock," I called, and pushed the door open with the toe of my shoe, balancing the coffees and bag of scones in my hand. "I come with gifts."

"Must be a peace offering because you sure didn't take up for me last night." The anger in her voice came through loud and clear. She sat behind the desk with papers scattered all over. She looked like she'd been up all night, which she probably was.

Her hair was pulled up in a scrunchie. Any piece of hair that wasn't long enough to pull back was tucked tight to her head with a bobby pin.

"I didn't know if you did or didn't kill her." I set the coffee and scones down. "After all, she was found dead with your scarf around her neck."

"You know that I didn't kill her." Her voice was just above a whisper. Her eyes drew across my face. "What earthly reason would I have?"

I avoided looking at her and picked up one of the cups and casually said, "So tell me about the interview." I wanted to get as much out of Fluggie as I could because maybe she had some sort of pertinent information she would consider unimportant.

"I got there and her assistant met me at the door. She let me in and Jade was lounged on the bed in some sort of old Hollywood movie star way. She had this turban on her head and a long silky robe that was neatly tied at her waist. She had on matching house slippers." Fluggie recalled the scene. There was really no need for her to tell me how Jade looked because ghost Jade was the same. "I asked her about growing up in a small town and how she got started in pageants and into acting."

Nothing seemed out of normal. Yet.

"Was the assistant there the whole time?" I asked, and mentally put Keisha on my list of people to see now that my day was suddenly wide-open.

"No." Fluggie walked around the office, busying herself with paperwork, and she continued, "It was just me and her. She did get a knock at the door and abruptly stopped the interview."

Fluggie walked over to the filing cabinet and slid open one of the metal drawers.

"Was it the assistant?" I asked, hoping I might have gotten my first clue.

"It wasn't her voice, but it was a woman's voice. Something about her hair." Fluggie glanced over her shoulder and looked at me. "She rushed me so fast I was only able to grab my cell phone off the little desk I was sitting at, leaving my tape recorder and scarf."

I leaned in a little closer to her. With her back to me, her voice was muffled.

"I got to my car and remembered my scarf." She pushed the metal drawer shut with a slam. "When I went back to retrieve it, she wasn't in her room and my scarf was gone along with my recorder." She eased her back up against the filing cabinet and crossed her arms. She looked at me with a glint of suspicion in her eyes. "And I know she didn't call you because I picked up her phone."

She reached deep into the front of her shirt and pulled a cell phone from her bra.

"This is her phone, which I had, and I know she didn't call you." She pinched the phone in between her finger and thumb and waved it in a slow manner.

Damn. Damn. Damn. Why on earth did I believe Jade Lee? I knew better. Even as a ghost she was full of crap just like she was while living.

"So that is why I called you here." She pushed herself off the file cabinet and slowly walked toward me. "I want to know what is going on."

Each step she took made my chest tense a little more. I wasn't good at lying and I was in a bit of a pickle.

"Okay. Fine." I sucked in a deep breath. "I know there is no way you killed her. That is not you, and you had no reason to kill her." I wrung my hands together. "When I pulled Jack into the closet, I told him that it's all circumstantial evidence that would never lead to an arrest. He knew it."

Her lips pursed. She wasn't buying it but I was going to keep selling it.

"I knew you couldn't kill anyone and I had to get out of there so we could put our heads together to figure out who set you up." I waited to see what she had to say.

"We did solve the last one together." I couldn't stand to wait a moment longer for her to respond. She was a tough nut to crack, but I knew I fractured her.

"My gut tells me something fishy is going on," she said.

I'd always heard about the keen intuition most reporters said they had and Fluggie definitely had it. I kept my lips pinched. I thought I'd done a pretty good job of covering my Betweener tracks.

"Look here." She flipped on the TV that hung on the wall. "I DVR everything that has to do with the news. Especially since I seem to be their number one suspect." The screen was already paused. "Have you ever heard of ghost orbs?"

She held the remote control in her hand and

pointed it at the TV. She pushed a button. The newsreel played.

"Right there!" She hit the pause button. The screen showed the front of the police station. "See that white round dot jumping around?"

"I'm famous," Jade squealed.

I moved closer and squinted.

"Mmmm, no." Slowly I shook my head.

"Right there." Fluggie jabbed the TV screen. "You can't tell me you don't see that white orb."

"Yes she does." Jade danced around. "I swear on my tiara she sees it."

"I think I need to call in one of those ghost hunter teams to look at these tapes." Fluggie was serious. Her voice held a tinge of excitement. "Think about it. They can talk to the ghost who I bet is Jade Peel. The ghost can tell them who killed her."

I gulped. My voice was shaky. "Don't be ridiculous." I had to think fast on my feet. "I've worked around dead people all my life and if anyone could see a ghost, it would be me. There is no such thing."

"Yes there is." Jade's voice carried unique force. "She's lying. She sees me."

"I don't know." Fluggie watched the DVR again. "My gut tells me I'm onto something with this." She shook the remote at the TV.

"My gut tells me that we need to look at the cell

phone and see what's on there. And we need to find your tape recorder and phone. The logical things." I sighed, trying not to bring too much attention to my churning stomach.

The last thing I needed was one of those ghost hunter people coming to town and seeing my Betweener client. Or worse. My Betweener client telling them that I could see ghosts too.

"I wonder if Jack Henry has your cell phone?" I questioned since she had Jade's. More importantly, I was trying to get Fluggie off the subject of calling in a ghost hunting team.

"And he'll just hand that over to you?" she asked, unconvinced.

"Probably not, but I can still ask him about it." Deep down I knew that I could somehow twist it around that Jade had said something about a tape recorder, or even ask Jade about it if she decided to show up when we were alone.

"I can't help but ask you if you were the one who killed Jade." There was a lethal glint in her eyes. "That is why I told you to come here." She paced back and forth. "First, you don't like Jade." She held her finger in the air. Then stuck up another finger like she was creating a list. "Second, you were eager to get me the interview. And third, it was convenient to put me at the scene after you killed her."

"First off,"—I was pretty offended she'd think that—"I was with Jack Henry on a date when you were interviewing her, and really, what kind of person do you think I am?"

"I have to cover all possibilities." She stared me down.

"I consider us friends and right now you could use one to help you." It wasn't like I exactly lied nor was it like we'd be having a slumber party and paint each other's nails, but in some sense we were friends. "If you honestly think I framed you for murder, I'll leave you alone to chase down leads by yourself. Or you can call your ghost hunter friends."

Fluggie laughed out loud. "Ghost hunters." She cackled louder. "What was I thinking? I might be losing my mind."

"No." My heartbeat started to settle down a little bit. "You are stressed."

Fluggie seemed to buy it.

"I will let my lawyer handle all the official stuff while I look into this." She picked up the cell phone and used her finger to scroll through whatever she had on the screen. "Here is a list of her outgoing calls." Fluggie pushed the piece of paper toward me. "I'm just now pulling her missed calls and she sure does miss a lot."

"I'm sure she's too busy or just is selective who

she talks to," I said. It seemed reasonable to assume that.

"And she only talks to Keisha and Patricia." Fluggie took the sheet from me and scribbled Patricia's name on it.

"Keisha is her assistant and Patricia is her stylist." I didn't see any reason why they should be suspicious. "What about an agent or someone?"

"There was a voice mail from a New York number that I've not listened to yet. The time stamp was about the time I left. So I wonder if it had anything to do with what happened." Fluggie used her fingers to play with the phone.

It was far-fetched that it would have something to do with Jade's murder, but no stone unturned, I reminded myself.

"Here." She set it down and the voice mail played.

The woman on the other end identified herself as Mookie. She went on to say that the production crew had told the producer about how much of a pain in the ass Jade had been in her hometown and the producer decided to pull the plug on the reality show. Mookie went on to tell Jade that if she didn't straighten up, her entire career was going to go up in flames. Plus she'd gotten an anonymous video of how badly she's acted while she's been in town.

Fluggie and I both sat stunned for a minute. As I listened, my sleuthing skills keyed in on who would send an anonymous video when there was a camera crew that had probably caught it all.

"Wait." I wondered. "Is that a landline from New York or a cell? Because if it is a cell then this Mookie doesn't have to be in New York."

"Good call." Fluggie picked up her old rotary phone on her desk and looked between Jade's cell and the numbers of her phone, carefully dialing the number. "Yes. Can you tell me if this is a landline? Um . . . kay." Fluggie wedged the phone between her ear and shoulder as she scribbled more next to Mookie's name. "Thank you."

"Well?" I asked.

"It's a landline for Hester and Hester Talent Agency. So this Mookie must be her agent." Fluggie held the phone out to me. "And you are the undertaker who is taking care of the funeral arrangements and would like to get a few words for the *Sleepy Hollow News* to go into her obituary."

"Oh no." I shook my head and waved my hand.

"What good is it to be an undertaker if you can't throw your weight around?" she asked. "Since we are good buddies and all." She winked, knowing she had pinned me up against the wall. "Or you could say you are with the Sleepy Hollow Police following up on the phone conversation from yesterday."

"Fine." I grabbed the phone. I'd much rather pretend to be someone and give a false name than have Jack get a call from Artie or this Mookie and have my name. Once Fluggie redialed the number, she hit the speaker button.

"Hi, I'm . . ." My mind did circles when I tried to formulate a made-up name. "Charlotte Zula." I said it really fast and winced when I put Charlotte's and Granny's names together. Probably not the best idea, but I went with it. "And I'm calling on behalf of the Sleepy Hollow Police."

Fluggie smacked her hand to her forehead. She continued to scribble down the conversation. "If I had my tape recorder, I could've recorded this," she whispered.

"And I'm doing a follow-up call about the voice message you left on Jade Lee Peel's cell phone about the cancellation of the television show." I stopped for a moment to collect my thoughts.

"What do you mean police?" The woman threw me for a loop; I didn't figure on any questions she might have.

"Ma'am, I regret to let you know that Ms. Peel was found dead in her guest room at the Sleepy Hollow Inn shortly after you called her." There was no other way to put it.

"Dead?" The woman gasped. "How did she die?"

"Ma'am, we are treating this case as a homicide until we can gather any more evidence, and your phone call to Ms. Peel could be a piece of the puzzle we are looking for." I looked up at Fluggie. She gave me a thumbs-up. "You are her agent, correct?"

"Yes I am." The woman fell silent. "Was."

"And you did confirm on the voice mail to Jade that the reality show deal was off the table." I wanted to make it clear, not only for me, but for Jack in case I had just stumbled upon something.

"Yes. She was supposed to make the town look like a hick town, not her look like a hick." Mookie didn't sound so happy with Jade's performance. "She's gone and done it." Mookie's voice was flat and almost cold. "I told her doctor that she'd make good on her promise."

"What promise was that?" I asked.

"Jade has spent the better part of the last two years in and out of mental facilities because she threatens to kill herself on a regular basis. And I wouldn't doubt it if she did kill herself over losing the reality deal. It was all she ever wanted. She couldn't wait to come back there for her little reunion and show your town how she made it big-time, when in reality her career has been floundering." Mookie's tone sounded more frustrated than sad.

"My scarf," Fluggie whispered as she made a pretend noose out of her hands and tugged on it as if she were hanging herself.

"I told her that she didn't need to leave the facility any sooner, but she insisted she had to go to this reunion and that was why she didn't have a team with her. Just that stupid assistant Keisha." Mookie was like the lock nine dam on the Kentucky River. I opened it and she flooded me with information. "Keisha follows her around like a little puppy. Followed her around," she corrected herself. "God, Keisha. How is she doing?"

"So let me get this straight." I had to make sure I heard everything correctly because if she did kill herself, why was she still here?

It wasn't like I was a pro at this Betweener gig. I'd only had five clients, and maybe she wasn't letting herself cross over until I gave Artie some peace and figured out why she'd do such a thing. And the mental institutions. Did he know about his daughter's state of mind?

"Yes, Officer." Mookie had fallen for my line of crap. "All of it's true."

After we said our good-byes and I had hung up, I looked at Fluggie.

"I think I need to go see Artie and see what he knew about his daughter. Plus give my sympathies to him." This was the part of the undertaker job I didn't like.

Talking to the family was always tough, but talking to a parent about their deceased child was altogether a different ball game.

"Why, do you think seeing him is going to help?" Fluggie asked.

"I think he might give us more details as to why she might have committed suicide or at least have knowledge like her agent did about her true unhappiness." Jade's face popped into my head.

She seemed like she had everything. It was like she had life by the you-know-whats. I really just wanted to go see Artie to see if her ghost would come back to me or if she did happen to cross over on her own if she had committed suicide.

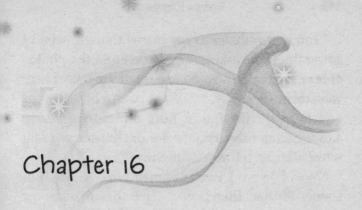

Chapter 16

Leaving the old mill didn't leave me one bit satisfied. I left with more questions than answers.

I stuck my earbuds in my ears and dialed up Jack Henry.

"Hey there." His deep voice dripped through the phone making me miss him even more.

"Good morning." I happily sighed and couldn't help but smile. "I'm guessing you were up all night?"

"You bet I was." He laughed. "You know me so well."

"Say." There was time for love later, but right now I was going to see what had happened to my Betweener client. "Do you think Jade Lee committed suicide?"

"You know, that was my initial thought when I got to the scene and saw her body and the photos of how the scarf was tied around her neck." There was doubt in his voice. "When I dug a little deeper and talked to Vernon a little more, it is clearly a strangling from the marks on the neck. Wait, why? Did she tell you something?"

"No." I knew I was going to have to tell him sooner rather than later. "She disappears for stretches and she's different than the other clients. She said she refused to go to the other side."

My other clients weren't able to go to the other side, and though I knew what the agent had told me, it seemed irrelevant if Vernon confirmed it was strangulation. Besides, Jack Henry will never find out I pretended to be Officer Charlotte Zula. I had said it so fast that Mookie had no time to catch the name.

"But we do know that if she was still here"—I meant ghost form and he knew it—"then Fluggie didn't kill her. When I met with Fluggie a few minutes ago, she was adamant about seeing an orb on the news and calling in a ghost hunting team."

"What?" Jack Henry wasn't following me. He sounded confused on the other end of the phone.

"Fluggie has pretty good intuition and she DVR'd all the news coverage on Jade and rightfully so since she's the obvious police suspect." Though Jack and I knew she didn't do it. "She insisted on calling in a ghost hunter."

"Oh," Jack said with caution. "You talked her out of it I hope."

"Don't worry." I put to rest any ideas he had in his head. "I think I did. But I did something you aren't going to be happy with."

"What?" His voice was thick and unsteady.

"Fluggie said that her interview with Jade was interrupted when someone knocked on the door. Jade made her leave immediately. Fluggie only had time to grab her phone and left behind her tape recorder." I kept both hands on the wheel and made sure to be careful on the country roads on my way back into town. "I called Jade's agent with Hester and Hester Talent Agency."

"I told you not to get involved unless it came up in conversation." Jack sighed with exasperation.

"How can I not?" I questioned. "Now I have to figure out where my ghost nemesis is too." I continued, "Anyways, not only did she tell me that the reality show Jade was filming while she was here was canceled because someone sent an anonymous video of her behavior while she was here and the camera crew told the producer about her behavior, but Jade just got out of a facility."

"What kind of facility?" he asked.

"Some sort of rehab because she's tried to kill herself several times." It sounded so awful coming out of my mouth. I began to feel sorry for Jade. She must've really had some issues in spite of looking like she had it all. "That's why I wondered if you ruled out suicide."

"We know she didn't, but if someone did commit suicide, would they still come to you?" he asked.

"I don't know." The Betweener gig was so new, I didn't have a clue. Initially I had thought it was just Eternal Slumber clients that had been murdered. Then I quickly found out it was anyone I knew that had been murdered. "The only thing I remember that psychic telling us was the more clients I got, the better my skills would become."

Jack had taken me to a psychic in Lexington after I had helped my first Betweener client. She confirmed my gift. The only problem was that she didn't know all the details or potential of my ability. I thought it would be possible for someone to commit suicide and be a client if their family needed closure. At this rate, anything was possible with this gift.

"What was the name of the agency again?" Jack asked. I knew it was a lead for him to follow up on. This was how we worked as a team for my Betweener clients. They gave me small details and he would put them together.

"Maybe I should go see Artie and see what he knew about Jade," I said after I had given him Mookie's information.

"I don't know." Jack contemplated, "He's pretty upset and I'm not sure he knew much about his daughter since she left town. I asked him all sorts of questions that he didn't know."

"I think I will go see him. Just to feel him out." My mind was made up.

"I'm not sure I like you sticking your nose into things with a murderer out there. I mean"—he let out a long sigh—"if the killer finds out that you are sticking your nose somewhere, then I'm worried they will come after you."

"I guess you are just going to have to keep an eye on me and protect me." I giggled.

"Emma Lee." Jack didn't find my comment so funny. "I'm not joking. Be careful."

"I'm kidding." I turned down the street that ran between Eternal Slumber and the town square. The network vans were still there. "When are these media people leaving?"

I had always loved looking at the pictures of the stars in the smutty, celebrity magazines while I stood in line at Artie's Meat and Deli. But all of this hoopla surrounding Jade's death was a little too much.

"Who knows." I could hear the irritation in his

voice. "They are here too. That's why I've got to go. I'm going to go back to the Inn and look for Fluggie's phone later this afternoon."

"Why don't we meet for lunch and discuss what you find out from Artie," he suggested, which was a good idea. Not only would I get a full belly, but I'd also get to look at Jack Henry while doing it. "I'll pick you up in a couple of hours."

"Sounds good." We said our good-byes and I stuck the phone back in my pocket.

When business was slow at the funeral home, John Howard always did odd jobs around town; right now I saw him across the street at the gazebo taking down the decorations for the parade and reunion. It was a shame too. The town was so looking forward to a fun time.

I ran inside the funeral home and straight to the kitchen. I opened the refrigerator door to see what I could whip up to take to Artie's. It was pretty bare. And what was in there looked to be a little old. I eyed the Arm & Hammer baking soda wondering what on earth I could make with that.

"What are you looking for?" Vernon stood behind me with a steaming cup of coffee. "I've made a pot of coffee if you want some." He gestured his cup toward the coffeepot.

"Thanks, but I'm looking for something to take to Artie's this morning so I can offer my condolences." I opened the crisper drawer. There was some wilted celery and carrots that were a little drawn and dried. I eyed the fat free Ranch dressing and the Ranch dressing; both bottles were turned on the tops with just enough in them to be combined.

I grabbed all of it (except the baking soda), knowing Granny would just die if she knew I was doing this. Deaths and funerals around Sleepy Hollow were just as much of a social gathering as a wedding. And you never came empty-handed. I mean food. My stomach growled and my mouth watered just thinking about the food I was sure the Auxiliary women had already taken to Artie.

Vernon's steel-blue eyes looked at me suspiciously. He tilted his head; his perfectly gelled salt-and-pepper hair stayed in place. He brought the cup of steaming coffee up to his lips and took a long calculated sip as he no doubt analyzed what I was doing.

"Don't judge me." I took a knife and cut the wilted spots off the celery and shucked down the dry parts of the carrots. "Business is slow."

He grinned his Hollywood smile and shook his head. Vernon was so debonair and reminded me of the old Hollywood movie royalty.

I grabbed a Tupperware bowl and combined the different bottles of Ranch dressing in it. There were plenty of serving trays in the pantry that we used for layouts and other funeral needs. I was able to use one and arrange the celery and carrots around the bowl of dressing. There were always leftover floral arrangements from different funerals that sat around the funeral home, some a little deader than others, but I found a few greenery sprigs and decorated the tray with them.

"Not bad." Vernon had planted himself in a chair and sipped his coffee as if I were his entertainment for the day. "I always said a woman can make anything beautiful."

"Why thank you." I stood back and looked at it myself. Pleased with the results. "So, tell me about Jade."

I swiped my finger across my phone and quickly text messaged Shirley from the Spare Time Country Cooking in Slicklizzard, Kentucky. It was a little diner located a little way from Sleepy Hollow that I had stumbled upon when I was working for my first Betweener client. I loved the food so much I'd asked Shirley if she'd cater the reunion. Now with the reunion canceled, I wasn't sure what to do with all the food.

"You know I can't do that." Vernon was right. If she were a client of Eternal Slumber, it would be a different story. "Seeing as my understanding is that Artie hasn't picked which funeral home he's using."

Too bad I didn't have some of Shirley's food to take to Artie right now, but it would be good for the repass, especially if I secured Jade's funeral today.

My eyes narrowed. My memory drew back to that awful day of my fateful run-in with Artie's plastic that slipped off the store's awning, knocking me flat-out cold. The only gift I got from Santa that year was the gift of seeing dead people, now Jade Lee Peel. In my eyes Artie Peel owed me.

Chapter 17

As death always came, so did the community. Artie lived in a small house behind Main Street, behind Artie's Meats and Deli. There were people everywhere. Hanging out on his front porch, leaning up against the tree in his front yard and talking over the small white picket fence. And a few were gathered around in a circle.

Curious, I walked up with my impromptu vegetable tray in my hand and the group of people parted like the Red Sea. Right in the middle was Granny in her full-length gown straddling her moped with her aviator goggles perched on top of her red head. A cameraman and a camera focused on her face.

"I've been twice widowed. Who can say that?"

Granny gave a wink to the camera. "And I got me a doctor on the line. Hook, line and sinker." She let out a little giggle and cast a fake fishing pole in front of her. "I've got a lot of stories to tell. Strange happenings as a funeral home director and owner. As well as the owner of Sleepy Hollow Inn. My life couldn't be more perfect for one of them TV reality shows." Granny looked up to the heavens and swept her arms wide out in front of her. "Zula Zooms." She twisted the throttle. The poor moped coughed. "Vroom!" Granny eyes caught mine.

I tried to slip back into the crowd.

"Emma Lee Raines!" Granny's voice lifted above the crowd. "Yep. Right on over there with that . . ." Granny's head bobbled back and forth trying to get a gander at what was in my hand. "What is on that Eternal Slumber tray?"

My lips pinched together in a thin smile. I could've killed her.

"Anyways. That's my Emma Lee, my granddaughter." Granny put her hand up to the side of her mouth as if she were going to whisper. She didn't. "She's got a case of the 'Funeral Trauma.' She thinks she sees dead people and no wonder since she's an undertaker. And if that don't make TV interesting, I don't know what does."

I darted around the group.

"Where are you going?" Granny hollered out. I waved my hand in the air and continued to walk. "Whoohoo! Emma! Oh well, forget her right now."

Granny went back to preaching why she should be considered for a TV reality show.

"Pastor Brown." I nodded when I walked through the door. Poor old Artie was sitting in the corner of his family room in his cracked, fake leather, brown recliner. "Charlotte Rae?" The shock of seeing my sister kneeling down by Artie nearly stopped my beating heart right then and there.

Then she'd have two clients instead of the one she was trying to get.

"Emma Lee." Artie stood up. "I'm so glad to see you, dear."

"Mr. Peel. I'm so sorry for your loss. Jade was such a kind soul." I hated to lie, but desperate times called for desperate measures. I was desperate for a client at the funeral home and desperate to find out where Jade had disappeared to since the preliminary results of her autopsy were strangulation, not suicide.

"You really aren't a good liar." Jade Lee's long thin leg swung back and forth from where she was perched up on the mantel of the fireplace. The pink pom-poms on the toe of her heels fluttered with each swing.

"Yes, such a wonderful soul." I tapped the frames on the mantel, each one of Jade in some sort of tiara and gown. I glared at her when I reached her at the end.

"Your sister sure does have a fantastic idea about all the amazing things funerals can be. Daddy will send me off in a horse-drawn Cinderella carriage." She squealed.

"I'll leave you with this." Charlotte patted Artie on the knee and pushed up to standing. "You know I'm here for you just like I've been with the rest of your family."

"Thank you, Charlotte." Artie nodded, his eyes hollow. "You've always been such a sweet girl."

"Such a snake," I murmured. "I'll go put this vegetable tray in the kitchen," I said when Charlotte Rae passed me.

"Oh, Emma." Charlotte Rae twisted around. Her long red hair curled in all the right places. Her lips were lined with the perfect shade of red to complement her green eyes. "It's business. Don't be going and flying off the handle."

"Business? I'm your sister. I live here." I couldn't believe it. "Does Granny know you are in here?"

"Why, yes." Charlotte crossed her arms and curled her fingers around her bony forearms. "In fact, I went to the Inn to talk about the sideboard and she was on her way over here. Two birds." She drummed her fingers.

"You think you're in high cotton with all the Cinderella horse-drawn carriage bit, but you don't fool me." I wasn't about to give her a tongue-lashing.

"How did you know about the carriage?" Charlotte unknotted her arms and planted her fists on her hips.

"It's all y'all do." I gulped. Shit. You'd think after five Betweener clients, I'd be able to distinguish what I can and can't say. That was an obvious can't.

"Um . . ." Charlotte's voice was velvet-edged and strong. "I've never had a Cinderella carriage. It was just sort of whispered in my ear when I walked in."

Damn, Jade Lee. I would bet my bottom dollar she whispered into Charlotte's ear.

"Whatever. You are my sister. You should stay in your own backyard." I jabbed my finger in her chest, wrinkling her fancy suit. "You barely waited until they moved her to the morgue . . . you . . ." I sucked in a deep breath and let it rip. "You are exactly like the kinds of undertakers Daddy called ambulance chasers."

"Don't you dare talk to me like that." Charlotte's temper flared.

"Just you remember," I warned, "the sun don't always shine on the same dog's tail all the time. I'll remember this."

"Stop this right now." Granny stood in the doorway of the kitchen door. The sun hit the sequins on her dress just right, blinding me in the right eye. "Y'all go on and mend fences. Y'all are sisters. Sisters!" Granny stomped. "Though a family rift would make good television." Granny contemplated the thought, then came to her senses. "But I won't stand for a family rift."

"Granny, she's come back to town to not only steal my sideboard but to steal my clients." I just didn't get where family loyalty was lost. "You always said family comes first. She's not my family."

"I'm not going to stand here and listen to this. I've got a Cinderella carriage to find." Charlotte turned on the balls of her high heels and trotted out like a horse, leaving me there to pick up the pieces.

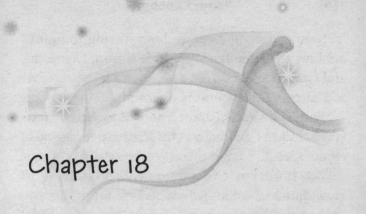

Chapter 18

"If I'd known you had such a nasty sister, I'd have been a lot nicer to you in school." Jade Lee sat on top of my sideboard. "And I wouldn't have given her the carriage ride idea for my funeral."

After Charlotte Rae had ruffled my feathers and I'd seen Jade Lee hadn't crossed over on her own, seeing Artie wasn't so important. I'd given my condolences and paid my respects. I'd gone to find Jade and did. Having her as an Eternal Slumber client was just the icing. For some reason, people died in seasons. Either I was busting out the seams with dead bodies or bone-dry.

"I knew Charlotte didn't come up with that on her own. Don't try to make up for it now," I growled and ran my hand across the sideboard.

I'd been staring at it for an hour, trying to figure out how to sneak it out and hide it from Charlotte and Granny. "Just do me a favor and hang around so I can get some answers out of you."

"Fine." She huffed and picked at her nails. "You know, I didn't get famous by letting people walk all over me."

"You think I'm letting them walk all over me?" How dare a ghost know what's best for me.

"I know they are," she said with a smug look on her face. "Didn't Charlotte give her part of the business over to you?"

"Yes."

"Wouldn't it be in the paperwork that everything she had was now all yours? Including this?" She ran her hand across the sideboard in a loving manner.

"Oh, Jade! If you were alive, I'd kiss you!" I jumped around and rushed to the office where I had filed the paperwork when we had dissolved our partnership.

"I'm not just beauty." She ghosted herself into the office and watched over my shoulder as I read the paperwork.

"You are right." I pointed to the clause that stated every piece of furniture and every piece of paperwork stayed with the funeral home. I licked my fingers and flipped the papers. My heart sank. I groaned.

"What?" Jade questioned, and stood over my shoulder.

"She hasn't signed the papers yet," I huffed. It was like pulling teeth for me to get Charlotte when she wasn't busy. I was tired of hearing her excuses of being busy and how she didn't want any part of the funeral home.

"You just need to go visit her and lay down the law." Jade pounded her fist in her other hand. "Get a spine." Jade Lee did her best to snap her fingers. "One day I'll be able to snap my fingers. I've been practicing." She tried a couple more times. "But you are being too nice. When you run a business, you have to take charge and know what is best or Burns and Hardgrove's is going to run you right out of town."

"You're right." All of a sudden I found a world full of confidence.

"I sure hope you are better at this Betweener job than the business side of Eternal Slumber because I'm getting a little antsy on this side. Maybe you should go see my dad again."

"Really?" I questioned whether or not Artie would be open to seeing me.

"Yes."

Her words of encouragement were all I needed to head back down to her dad's and get him to make the decision to have Jade's funeral at Eternal Slumber. Then head over to Hardgrove's and force Charlotte Rae's hand.

The crowd inside had died down and a few stragglers were hanging on the porch with a glass of Granny's iced tea she'd brought over.

"If I'd known the trouble it would've caused." The bags under Artie's eyes showed his sadness. He had a photo of a younger Jade Lee gripped in his hands. "Her first pageant win."

"Do you mean you wouldn't have put her in pageants?" I asked, trying to understand what he was saying to me.

"For years I'd been trying to get Jade to come home. She refused. She wanted so badly to make something of herself." His head dropped. "I tried to be a good dad to her. I probably should've gotten remarried and given her a mamma."

I rubbed his back for some comfort. It was part of the undertaker job that was a fine line. People liked to be comforted differently when they were hurting.

"She'd battled so many demons. In and out of those rehabs." So he knew about Jade and her problems.

He put his head in his hands and silently cried.

His shoulders bobbed up and down as the grief swept over him.

"I knew that she was going to see Mary Anna at the spa to get her hair done, so I slipped into Girl's Best Friend and put Clorox in all of those dye bottles." He glanced up at me. "If she didn't have that reality show, she probably would've come home where she belonged. If I would've left well enough alone."

My mouth dropped. I quickly looked at my watch.

"If Jade were here, she'd forgive you," Tina said, trying to make him feel better. "You were a great father to her and she loved you." Tina gave him a reassuring smile. "I'll get you a glass of Zula's iced tea she brought over. It will make you feel better."

Tina left the room.

"I do love you, Daddy." Jade stood behind his chair. Her hands rested on top of his shoulders.

The corners of his eyes dropped. "I sent a mashed-up video of her behavior to her agent. Some of it was taken from my cell phone and other parts were taken from the security cameras outside the deli. I sent it anonymously so she'd never find out it was me."

"Oh, you didn't, Daddy." Jade Lee ghosted herself in front of her father with her mouth wide-open. "Why?" She fumed.

She got that look in her eye that she'd gotten when Keisha had handed her the mirror at Girl's Best Friend. It wasn't a good look. She looked like her insides were boiling and at any minute her head was going to pop off like the lid of a pressure cooker.

"I can't help but think I had something to do with this." His chin fell to his chest.

"Mr. Peel." Tina Tittle walked in with a glass of iced tea. "Here is your tea."

I gave her an appreciative smile. "It's kind of you to be here."

"Gracious me, why on earth wouldn't I be?" Tina asked. "Jade was just like my sister and Artie is just like my dad."

He mustered up a grateful smile.

"Now it's more important than ever to figure out who killed me." Jade Lee stood between her father and best friend. "Look at them. No peace until the killer is brought to justice."

"Please let me know if I can do anything for you. You know I'm here to host her funeral if you'd like to use Eternal Slumber's services." I hated to drum up business this way, but I wanted to beat Charlotte Rae at her own game.

With a quick good-bye, I hurried out of Artie's house and up to Main Street, taking a right, barreling down to Girl's Best Friend Spa. I knew I had to right his wrong no matter how crazy I looked.

"Where do you think you are going? You have to find out who killed me and now!" Jade's high heels clicked as she scurried behind me.

I ignored her and flung the door open to the spa. The beauty shop was packed.

"Hi, Emma." Mary Anna Hardy had completely channeled Marilynn Monroe. Her hair fell across her head in large blond curls. Her mile-long black lashes curled plum up to her brows. Her tight, cropped white jeans had big red kissy lips all over them with a red sleeveless button-up shirt with ruffles waving down the front tucked taut into the waistband of her jeans.

"Hello." I strutted over to her. My eyes zeroed in on the clear ketchup-looking bottle filled with a gray liquid that she was holding in her plastic gloved hand. I sucked in a deep breath and got ready to prepare for my "Funeral Trauma" performance.

Mary Anna jumped back, her mouth dropped. "What is wrong with you?"

"I'm feeling like you shouldn't be doing any sort of hair coloring since you turned poor Jade Lee's hair green." I let out an evil groan to help me play the part.

I ran back to the back where I knew she kept

all the bottles of dye and quickly unscrewed the bottles one by one, pouring the contents out into the sink.

"Emma Lee! Stop it!" Mary Anna's long finger-nails clicked on the screen of her phone. No doubt in my mind she was calling the authorities. "You are going to pay me back for these." She tried to plant her body between me and the last couple of bottles. "Someone call the sheriff and call Zula Fae!"

"No more dye jobs!" I screamed, shoving her to the side and grabbing the last of the bottles.

There was no time to dump them, so I ran out of the back room with a sack full of hair dye and out the front door of the shop.

"What on earth is wrong with you?" Granny's moped skidded to a stop in front of me, cutting me off. "Give me the bottles." Granny gestured for them.

"No." I held my arms above my head.

"Emma Lee Raines, rein in the crazy." Granny jerked the moped up on the stand and threw her leg over the seat. The sequins made a trickle sound as the dress shimmered down her small frame when she stood. "Give me those."

"No," I protested.

"Right now!" Mary Anna fussed.

"I'll take those." Artie came out of nowhere. "And I'm going to come clean."

"You don't have to." I was willing to protect him and Mary Anna.

"What are you two talking about?" Mary Anna put her hands on her hips.

"I was the one who sabotaged your color for my daughter's hair." Artie's voice lowered. "I knew that she was coming to see you to get her hair done and she was bringing the camera crew. I didn't want her to make that reality show and I knew she'd be upset if you messed up her hair color. So . . ." Artie's chest heaved up and down. He grabbed one of the bottles from my hand. "I broke into your shop and put Clorox in these. All of them."

"And I was trying to not only keep him out of it by pretending to be a little kooky, but also trying to protect you from doing any more bad dye jobs and ruining your business by dumping out all the bottles." It was probably a better idea that I had just come clean with her, but I didn't want Artie to get in trouble for breaking and entering. "Don't you think he's been through enough?" I asked, playing on Mary Anna's sympathetic side.

"I won't press charges if you let me do Jade's hair." Mary Anna grabbed the bottles from Artie's hands. "I've had a handful of cancellations because of the situation you created."

"And if she does her hair, that means you have

to host Jade's funeral at Eternal Slumber because she works for me." I shrugged.

Granny's lips quirked up into a small smile. She winked.

Mmm-hmm . . . I thought about Charlotte Rae. Two could play this game. She'd be so mad if I got Jade's body. The only reason she wanted to host her funeral was for the celebrity status and free publicity.

"And I'll be more than happy to get one of Dottie Kramer's horses and a carriage for a beautiful graveside ceremony," I added in.

"Well." Artie bit his lip.

"Daddy!" Jade Lee appeared. "You can't let her get one of Dottie's broke-back horses. That is a disgrace. A disgrace!" Jade stomped. "You already disgraced my hair. And Dottie wasn't nice to me when Tina and I saw her at the Buy-N-Fly."

"It will be amazing," I assured him, ignoring her, but keeping her comment about Dottie Kramer tucked in a spot in my mind.

"I sort of told Charlotte Rae I'd think about her services." Artie wrung his hands together.

"Don't you worry about Charlotte Rae." I grinned because I couldn't wait to see the look on her face when I told her I had secured the funeral of Jade Lee Peel.

Jack Henry pulled up in his cruiser. He got out and stuck his sheriff's hat on his head.

"Ladies." He nodded all professional like, sending goose pimples all over me. "Artie."

"Jack to the rescue." Jade batted her lashes and gushed over Jack.

"Geesh," I muttered under my breath. Jack looked at me. The crease between his brows deepened.

"Well?" Mary Anna nodded; her eyebrows rose as she looked at Artie to get his answer.

Artie didn't hesitate. It was obvious that Mary Anna had called the sheriff when I was doing my "Funeral Trauma" stint and he was here to collect the crazy. Only the crazy, me, had protected Artie Peel.

"Deal!" Artie stuck his hand out.

"We won't be needing your services, Sheriff." Mary Anna tucked the tainted bottles up under her armpit and hurried on inside.

"Emma, I'll bring those papers by and leave them at Eternal Slumber. I'm hoping we can have the funeral tomorrow afternoon." Artie had made a definite decision.

"I'll take good care of her," I promised him.

"You better be dolled up for my funeral. Not that regular old black suit you keep in that closet of your office," Jade warned. "I saw it in there and that's about depressing and boring."

I cleared my throat. Jack Henry looked at me the way he did when he knew a Betweener client was around. He was good at reading my body language.

"Thanks, Artie. I'll be in touch if I need to be." I would take care of everything now. "The only thing I need from you will be an outfit to dress her in."

"Oh." Artie looked pained. "I'll ask Tina to pick something out. If it were left up to me, I'd stick her in something she'd be so embarrassed to wear."

"Oh, Daddy. I hate he has to go through this," Jade cried out. "He did this with Mamma and I had to watch him. Now me. Emma Lee, you have to find my killer."

"Just have her bring it over to the funeral home," I suggested. "The sooner the better."

Artie said his good-byes.

I turned to Granny.

"Listen, I need you to go to Hardgrove's with me after I get finished here for a quick chat with Charlotte Rae. She has yet to sign off on the transfer of papers and I can't keep having funerals with her on the paperwork." I held on to that confidence Jade had given me and laid down the law like she said. "I need you to back me up."

"I have a lot of pies to make for this repass of

Jade's." Granny didn't even have to have me ask her to make food for the get-together after Jade's funeral. It was automatic that the Auxiliary women would take care of all the food needs.

"You have all night," I told her.

"Fine. But I ain't gonna like it." Granny had yet to go see the Hardgrove's Legacy Center. "It just ain't natural." Granny fussed about the big funeral home that celebrated more than just helping the dead enter into the Kingdom.

Granny revved up her moped and took off toward the Inn.

"Since we are here, let's go inside and question Mary Anna," I suggested. "Afterward, I have to go see Charlotte and I'm taking Granny with me. I looked at my papers today and she still hasn't signed them."

"When you get back, we can meet for our lunch." Jack Henry was so understanding. "Let's see what Mary Anna has to say."

When Jack opened the door to the spa, the chattering women didn't seem to be such chatty Cathies. Everyone's eyes were on me as if my crazy button was about to go off.

"Everything is fine now." I put my hands out in front of me, assuring them I wasn't about to explode like I had a few minutes ago. "Where is Mary Anna?"

One of the stylists pointed back to the wood door where square gold letters read OFFICE. Jack knocked on the door. Mary Anna called out for us to come in.

"Now what?" She was clicking away on the calculator and cussing under her breath.

"Are you okay?" I asked.

"No. I'm not." She clicked some more. "Jade had rented out the entire spa. I had my stylists cancel their clients because Jade told me she would cover the cost of the canceled appointments. After her hair got messed up, she refused to pay for any of the time." She threw her hands up in the air and fell back in her chair. "Now I don't know what to do. I don't have enough money to pay them all for a full day of canceled clients."

"I guess that made you mad about Jade not paying you." Jack Henry thought he was sly about his line of questioning, but I knew where he was going with it.

"Mad? Furious." Her face turned red answering Jack's question. I could only imagine how she felt yesterday.

"Enough to have killed Jade?" Jack asked.

"Jack Henry Ross!" she yelled in a high-pitched voice. "Have you lost your ever-loving mind? I most certainly would never kill someone over money. You have the wrong Hardy."

She was right. Unfortunately, her brother was sent to prison for just that—killing their father over a bet gone bad.

"I was with my mamma at Sleepy Hollow Baptist playing Friday night bingo. B-I-N-G-O." she spelled it out as if Jack didn't know how to spell.

He was writing down everything she was saying.

"I'm not saying you killed anyone, but I have to follow up on anyone who argued with Jade and your fight was pretty public." Jack got up and I followed his lead. "Thanks for answering my questions."

"You're welcome." She didn't bother seeing us out; she went back to clicking away on the calculator. "Emma, I'll be over early in the morning to do Jade's hair."

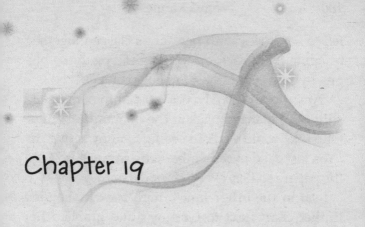

Chapter 19

"Lawzy bee." Granny scooted to the edge of the chair and lifted her arms in the air like she was in Sunday morning worship at Sleepy Hollow Baptist and she just got the spirit or something. But we weren't sitting in church, we were in Charlotte Rae's office.

I sucked in a deep breath, preparing myself for whatever was going to come out of Granny's mouth. She'd been a ball of Southern spitfire the entire way here. Quite frankly, I was surprised I even got her here. Especially with the repass happening tomorrow. She had a lot of food to prepare.

"Please, please, please let me die before anything happens to Emma Lee." Her body slipped down the fancy, high-back mahogany leather chair as she fell to her knees with her hands clasped together, bringing them back up in the pleading-to-the-big-guy-in-the-sky motion. "I'm begging you."

"Are you nuts?" My voice faded into a hushed stillness. I glanced back at the door, in fear Charlotte Rae would walk in seeing Granny acting up. "You just need to remember why we are here. Sign the papers so I can keep the sideboard."

I sat in the other fancy, high-back mahogany leather chair next to Granny's and grabbed her by the loose skin of her underarm. "Get back up on this chair before Charlotte Rae gets back in here."

"What?" Granny quirked her eyebrows questioningly. "I do want to die before something happens to you. I can't imagine my corpse being in a big ole place like this."

"That is exactly why I need her to sign the papers. If she has any stake in Eternal Slumber when you croak, she will try to move your body. I'm telling you." I had resorted to using scare tactics with Granny. "We aren't here to talk about your death. So focus, Granny." I gave her the two-finger gesture pointing between our eyes. "Tell Charlotte to sign the papers."

"Well, I ain't lying! I do hope and pray you are the granddaughter that will be doing my funeral, unless you get a flare-up of the 'Funeral Trauma.'"

She sucked in a deep breath and got up off her knees. She ran her bony fingers down the front of her cream sweater to smooth out any wrinkles so she'd be presentable like a good Southern woman—apparently forgetting she was just on her knees begging for mercy a second ago.

I was glad she at least dumped the gown and looked a bit normal.

"Flare-up?" I sighed with exasperation. "It's not like arthritis."

The "Funeral Trauma."

"I'm fine," I huffed, and took the pamphlet off Charlotte Rae's desk, keeping my gift to myself.

"You are not fine." Granny rolled her eyes. "People are still going around talking about how you talk to yourself." She shook her finger at me. "If you don't watch it, you are going to be committed. Surrounded by padded walls. Then . . ." She jabbed her finger on my arm. I swatted her away with the pamphlet. "Charlotte Rae will have full control over my dead body and I don't want someone celebrating a wedding while my corpse lies in the next room."

I opened the pamphlet and tried to ignore Granny the best I could.

"Do you hear me, Emma Lee?" Granny asked. I could feel her beady eyes on me. "Don't you be disrespecting your elders. I asked you a question."

"Granny." I placed the brochure in my lap and reminded myself to remain calm. Something I did often when it came to my granny. "I hear you. Don't you worry about a thing. By the time you get ready to die, they will have you in the nut house alongside me," I joked, knowing it would get her goat. "And a good way not to worry about it is to have Charlotte sign the papers."

The door flung open and the click of Charlotte Rae's high-dollar heels tapped the hardwood floor as she sashayed her way back into her office. She'd changed since we saw her an hour or so ago.

The soft green linen suit complemented Charlotte's sparkly green eyes and the chocolate scarf that was neatly tied around her neck. It was the perfect shade of brown to go with her long red hair and pale skin.

"I'm so sorry about that." She stopped next to our chairs and looked between me and Granny. She shook the long loose curls over her shoulders. "What? What is wrong, now?"

"Granny is all worried I'm going to get sent away to the nut house and you are going to lay her out here." The words tumbled out of my mouth.

"I . . ." Granny's mouth opened and then snapped shut. Her face was as red as the hair on her head. "I meant that I didn't want to be placed at Burns Funeral. I don't know what they do down in their morgue."

"Granny. Remember we talked about the cremation." Charlotte Rae eased her toned hiney on the edge of her desk and rested upon it. "Here at Hardgrove's we offer a full line of services. It's the way of the future."

Was she giving us her sales pitch? My jaw clenched. My eyes narrowed. I glared at her perfectly lined hot pink lips. With Charlotte's coloring, she did look great in pink. Heck, she'd look great in a burlap sack. I tucked a strand of my long, dull brown hair behind my ear and folded my hands in my lap with my short bitten-off nails tucked in. She spent a lot of money at the nail salon, getting the perfect manicure and it did look good.

But she looked a little tired. Not normal for Charlotte.

"Well, that certainly wasn't the answer I expected to hear." I shook my head. Since Charlotte had left as my co-owner of Eternal Slumber Funeral Home, I had been left in charge of everything and I was beginning to forget how bossy she was, until now. "Nor does Granny want to be cremated. Right, Granny?" I nudged Granny.

"I'm sorry, Emma Lee." Charlotte crossed her arms over top of her chest. Her brows lifted. Her

green eyes lit up a little. "Did I hurt your feelings?"

"No"—my voice hardened ruthlessly—"but
you could at least say that I'm not crazy and for
Granny to stop being ridiculous."

I grabbed my purse off the floor and pulled out
the envelope with the legal papers Charlotte had
to sign to make her desertion of the family business official and make sure I would keep my sideboard. Not that Hardgrove's Funeral Home was
much competition since it was in the neighboring
town, Lexington, Kentucky.

But it was just like Charlotte to up and leave
when times get lean. So lean that I hadn't been
sure I was going to be able to pay John Howard,
Mary Anna and Vernon. When clients that had
already made preneed funeral arrangements with
Eternal Slumber started pulling out because they
didn't want the "Funeral Trauma" girl to handle
them in death, Charlotte Rae jumped ship. She
took a job with Hardgrove's Funeral Homes at
their Lexington location.

Since they were in Lexington, a good forty minutes away from Sleepy Hollow, they really weren't
our competition. But family was family. And in a
small town, family stuck together. Not Charlotte.
She bailed, leaving me with all the chips to pick
up. And *that* was exactly what I have done.

"I don't think Granny is being ridiculous. I mean . . ." Charlotte picked up one of the same brochures I still had in my lap and gave it a good, swift flick. It unfolded like an accordion. "Here at Hardgrove's we are a full-service center." Her pink fingernail pointed to the first photo. "We offer a full line of funeral services with a state-of-the-art facility. Not like the ones in Sleepy Hollow." And there was the dig about where we grew up.

"You mean Eternal Slumber without saying it?" I wasn't going to let her get away with saying we weren't meeting the needs of our residents. I had yet to tell her that Artie had decided to have Jade laid to rest using Eternal Slumber. That loosely means the same as having his arm twisted behind his back so Mary Anna didn't press charges against him.

I decided to keep my little secret about Jade in my back pocket in fear Charlotte would get mad and not sign the papers.

"No, no." She shook her head and wagged her finger at me like I was some child. "There is also Burns Funeral." As if I didn't know the only other funeral home in Sleepy Hollow, my direct competitor. "They are definitely no longer top-of-the-line since O'Dell was elected Sleepy Hollow's mayor."

"Do tell." Granny lit up like a morning glory;

she was tickled pink to hear any and all gossip concerning O'Dell Burns since he beat her in the election by only two votes.

O'Dell's sister, Bea Allen moved back to town to take over the funeral home while O'Dell spent all his time in his plush office at the courthouse. I hadn't seen her since Jade passed and wondered if this little bit of information was why.

"This is on the down-low." Charlotte gave the good ole Baptist nod that meant we were supposed to keep our mouths shut because she was about to give us some deep-fried small town gossip, but she obviously forgot she was talking to Granny. "I have had several of Burns's customers come here and change their preneed funeral arrangements."

"They have?" Granny put her hand to her chest and sucked in. "Who?"

Granny's response should've been, why didn't they come see Emma Lee? Which was my question too.

"I'm not going to say, but let me tell you that I heard they put the wrong clothes on the wrong corpse." Charlotte Rae's grin was as big as the Grand Canyon. Granny clapped in delight like a little kid getting a piece of candy, turning my stomach in all sorts of directions at the sight. "Since I know you won't tell . . ." Charlotte Rae leaned in and whispered, "Old man Ridley died and he was in some branch of the armed services. His family insisted he be buried in his hat. Also, Peggy Wayne was laid out in the room next to old man Ridley and her family wanted to make sure her family pearls were buried with her. When Ridley's widow got there, he had on Peggy Wayne's pearls and Peggy had on Ridley's hat. Ridley's widow jerked the hat off Peggy's ice-cold body, taking her wig with it."

Granny gasped in horror, only there was a twinkle in her eye of joy that shone brighter than a flashlight, encouraging Charlotte Rae to continue her horrid tale.

"Needless to say, it spread all over the gossip circles and here I am today." She patted the files behind her on the desk. "Working up new contracts."

"Why didn't you send them to Emma Lee?" Granny asked. I was a bit relieved to see she was getting her wits about her.

"I'm not going to turn down business." Charlotte cackled. "I have to make a quota here in order to get my big bonus."

"The Grim Reaper must be busy because Emma Lee's got 'em lined up four dead bodies deep waiting to be buried," Granny lied. "There's gonna be a lot of good eating coming up that's for sure."

Although Granny was flapping her jaws way too much, my mouth did water at the thought of the repass. That was one great thing I loved about our small Southern Kentucky town, funerals were just as big a social gathering as a wedding. And all the locals put their differences aside to come together, bringing food and giving respect to the deceased. The repass was the meal after the funeral service. And Granny always brought homemade apple or cherry pie. Mmm, mmm, I could taste her buttery crust as if I was eating a piece.

"Is that right, Emma Lee? Business is good?" Charlotte asked, bringing me out of my food dream. There was an element of surprise on her face. "Too bad you aren't in the running for Jade Lee Peel. I'm sure we'll get a lot of press."

"You are talking out of turn." Granny was about to spill her guts about Jade being laid out at Eternal Slumber.

"Now, Granny." It was time. I put the envelope in front of Charlotte. "Granny is exaggerating." I pointed to the envelope. "Here is the paperwork for you to sign over Eternal Slumber to me. It isn't right that you haven't signed these yet. You are working here and I'm down in Sleepy Hollow. Sign the papers."

Charlotte Rae took it and carefully lifted the envelope flap. Gingerly she took the papers out and unfolded them, taking a glance at them.

"I'll look them over later." She folded them back up and stuck them back in the envelope.

"Later? How much later?" I demanded to know. "There is nothing in there but you giving up your half of the funeral home. You said you were done and it needs to be final."

"Calm down, Emma Lee." Charlotte patted her palms down to the ground. "I'm going to sign them, but I want to show Granny around before it gets busy in here."

In my head, I jumped up and grabbed Charlotte by her long hair, flung her to the ground—breaking one of her nails of course—and forced her to sign the papers. In reality, I swallowed my pride, got up, grabbed the envelope off her desk and followed her and Granny out of the office.

"Here is where we host the receptions." Charlotte took us into a room filled with round tables and chairs. There was a serving buffet at the front of the room. The room was painted a pale yellow with dark brown crown molding and chair rail. The carpet was maroon with subtle yellow flecks that matched the walls. Pictures on the wall were paintings of retired Keeneland horses that probably cost more than I'll ever make throughout my entire life.

"For the funerals or the weddings?" Granny

was getting caught up in the pageantry of the big funeral home center.

"We do not have repasses here at Hardgrove's." Charlotte gestured around the room with her hands like she was one of those models on *The Price Is Right*. "We have a catered chef who prepares fruit trays, cheese plates and small dessert options, along with tea or coffee. We call the get-together a celebration of life. Weddings are a celebration. Babies are a celebration. Parties are celebrations, and funerals are celebrations of life."

"Why do you need a chef for that?" I questioned, trying to find anything to make Charlotte look bad. "Seems to me that is a lot of wasted money when the women in the community like to cook."

Charlotte ignored me and continued telling Granny about how they also use it for wedding receptions along with any other celebration they could think of.

"We have a lot of baby showers." Charlotte squeezed her shoulders up to her ears in delight. "I just love those."

"Baby showers?" Granny drew back. All five foot four inches of her small frame froze. "Charlotte Rae, didn't we raise you better than that?"

Granny's insecurities were showing. It was true. Charlotte and I were raised in the family living

area of the funeral home right alongside Granny.
Granny, Momma and Daddy ran the funeral home
while Charlotte and I tried to lead a normal life,
only sleeping in a bed in the next room over from
a dead body was far from normal. Jade Lee Peel
had been good at reminding everyone of just how
not normal it was.

Charlotte up and left after I got the "Funeral
Trauma" because everyone in town started switch-
ing their preneed funeral arrangements to Burns
Funeral when they thought I was going nuts.

I had regained a few of the lost clients after
Charlotte left me to take this big undertaker job
at Hardgrove's. And a few new clients, like Jade.

"Oh, Granny, you raised me fine. Times have
changed and so does business." Charlotte pish-
poshed Granny. She continued to show us around
the large building, going on and on about how
they have had retirement parties, birthdays and
christenings.

"Christenings?" Granny snickered. "You mean
to tell me I could go over here to see my dead
relative and walk over yonder to see my great-
grandbaby get christened all in one day?"

Charlotte ignored Granny and continued on
with the grand tour.

"I really would like to you sign these papers." I
held the envelope out in front of Charlotte when

we walked down the hall to get a look at one of the viewing rooms.

Charlotte skipped around me, not giving any acknowledgment to the papers I practically shoved in her face.

"Shh." Granny batted my hand away and followed right behind Charlotte.

I sucked in a deep breath and tucked a piece of my hair behind my ear, ran my hand down my white T-shirt before I gave in, once again, and followed them to the next room.

The next room looked more like a banquet hall than a viewing room. Large round tables dotting the entire room had crisp baby-blue tablecloths over them and had at least ten chairs around each of them. White taffeta material was stretched and tied around the backs of each chair with a big stiff bow on the back.

"There you are!" A woman jumped out from behind a large stereo speaker from across the room. And then lickety-split, she was snapping her fingers and pointing at Charlotte Rae. "My Candy doesn't deserve a fine wedding reception where the flowers smell like those of a funeral!" She put her hands on her hips and turned to me. Her dirty blond hair was clipped short and her black roots were creeping out from her skull. "Can you smell that?" she asked me with a demanding tone. "Death. That is what I smell. And I told my Candy I wasn't going to have a dead body next to my princess as she cut that cake I paid an arm and a leg for. Do you hear me?" she rambled on, not giving Charlotte a chance to even speak.

"I understand." Charlotte Rae tried to calm the woman down.

"No you don't or this would not be happening." The woman gave Charlotte a stern look. "This is an outrage and you better fix it or another one of them rooms will be filled out there!"

"I will take care of it, Melinda." A crimson color crept up the back of Charlotte's neck. In true Charlotte Rae Southern charm, she gave Melinda a smile that didn't quite reach her eyes, and said, "I promise, your Candy will have the wedding of her dreams."

"Her dreams?" Melinda let out a big fit of laughter with a cough. "Hell, she ruined her dreams when she laid down with the Denise boy. But it ain't no skin off my nose, because I told her I wasn't gonna raise no more youngin's. Not even my grandbabies."

Granny's eyes darted between Charlotte and Melinda. A delightful grin spread over her face. Charlotte had her hands full and Melinda was giving her a run for her money.

"Momma! You stop talking about us." The

shrill voice echoed through the room. A woman who must've been Princess Candy stood in the doorway with a scrawny-looking boy. Candy's black hair was permed to death. She grabbed the boy's hand and bustled over to us, practically dragging him like a rag doll. "She ain't never been happy for me. She's the one who insisted on all this!"

Candy dropped the boy's hand and stuck her nose up in the air. She took a few quick sniffs. The boy must have been the Denise boy. Poor guy. I felt sorry for him. He didn't look older than eighteen. He was shorter than the princess and he was in desperate need of a haircut, his curls unfurled all over the top of his head.

"You smell that?" Princess Candy smacked the Denise boy with the backside of her hand before she planted her hands on her hips, causing her baggy shirt to become taut, exposing the outline of what looked to be a pregnant belly. "Death!"

A groan escaped from Charlotte's lips.

"I told you that this place smelled like dead people. Are you trying to piss me off?" Candy came nose to nose with Melinda.

Melinda's arms flew up in the air. "See, I told you!" She pointed to Charlotte and then faced the Denise boy. "Boy, she's gonna rip your heart right out of you, fry it up and eat it on a biscuit and swallow it down with a big swig of iced tea if you don't run."

"Fix this!" Candy grabbed the boy's hand and flung him toward the door, dragging him all the way out. "Or someone will take the fall for this!"

"Fix what?" Gina Marie Hardgrove, owner of Hardgrove's Legacy Centers, walked into the event room carrying a tray of glasses filled with sweet tea and finger sandwiches, dodging the lovebirds. "Oh my!" Gina placed the tray on the table before she gave Granny a hug. "Zula, it's been so long." She held Granny out at arm's length, getting a good look at her. I couldn't stop looking at that big, baseball-sized diamond on her finger. "You haven't changed a bit. And this one." Gina let go of Granny and patted Charlotte on the back. "She is such an asset to Hardgrove's. I really am sorry we stole her from you." She gave me a wink.

In the South, a wink speaks volumes and Gina Marie's was more of a dig than a compliment. Memories of Gina Marie flooded over me. As a kid we would see the Hardgroves at different funeral conventions and all us kids would hang out together. Then there was mortuary school. Gina Marie was there with me and Charlotte. That damn ring of hers was why I got a C-minus in the class. I spent most of my days dreaming of having one.

"Now I can go and visit our other centers knowing I'm leaving here with our Lexington center in good hands." Gina Marie nodded over to Charlotte, who had gingerly taken Melinda aside and was talking to her in the corner of the room.

"I guess we better go." Granny tugged on my arm.

"When you get a moment, can you please have Charlotte sign the papers?" I handed them to Gina Marie.

"She still hasn't signed these?" Her face turned white and a scowl swept over her features. "She did sign a noncompete with us, so I'm going to have to take this up with her."

Charlotte left Melinda in the corner and joined us, jerking the envelope from Gina Marie's hand. "It has nothing to do with a noncompete," she assured Gina Marie before turning toward me and Granny and gesturing for us to get the heck out of there.

A small stab hit my heart as Charlotte Rae quickly recovered from the embarrassing scene with a warm smile. Something I was never able to compete with.

"It was so good of you to come by. Emma Lee, I'll get these back to you soon." She waved the envelope in the air. "I must get back to work. Unlike Eternal Slumber, we are always busy with a life event. Yoo-hoo, Arley!" Charlotte raced over to one of the gardeners in the front of the funeral home. "You need to put the ducklings in the fountain!"

There was no reason to fuss with her because she wasn't going to listen and Granny had already started off toward the car. I recognized Arley Burgin, Hardgrove's grave digger and evidently lawn boy, standing in the fountain with bright yellow gloves clear up to his elbow and a scrub brush in one of his hands. I didn't know Arley all that well, but he was on the men's softball team that was sponsored by Eternal Slumber. He had mentioned he wasn't a fan of Gina Marie, which tickled me pink and by the look on his face, he wasn't a big fan of Charlotte either.

"Oh my stars." Granny got into the passenger side of the hearse and buckled up. "That was a sight for sore eyes."

I started the engine and pretended to adjust the rearview mirror when I was really looking back at Charlotte. It was good Southern manners to stand outside and wave by as someone pulled off in their car, but bad luck to watch them completely drive off. When we were almost out of sight, Charlotte stomped her feet and hurried back into Hardgrove's.

"I'm a little disappointed in how she reacted

to that nasty woman." Granny sat poised with her hands in her lap. "She should've told her that there were a few funerals being held and the flowers would be removed way before the wedding." Granny lifted her hand and nervously tapped her finger on the door handle. "Who on earth ever heard of opening a place like that?"

"Really?" I gripped the wheel, turning down the road that took us right back home to Sleepy Hollow where we belonged. "The fact that she hasn't signed the paperwork should be what you can't believe. I mean, she's working illegally for Gina Marie. And she still has claim to my sideboard."

"Pish-posh." Granny brushed me off. "She's not happy there. I can see it in her eyes. It's just a matter of time before she comes back to Eternal Slumber. Mark my words, that is why she hasn't signed those papers. And don't you worry." Granny patted my arm. "My preneed arrangements are at Eternal Slumber. Cremated? Who ever heard of such?"

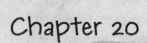

Chapter 20

And to top it all off"—I sucked down a gulp of Diet Coke to wet my whistle—"she still refused to sign the papers."

"I'm sorry, Emma." Jack put his hand across the table at the Inn's restaurant. He had been waiting for me when Granny and I pulled up. "Do you think she does want to come back?"

"I don't see why. We don't have all that high-and-mighty stuff she bragged about." I took another long sip through the straw before I got to the bottom of the glass and slurped what liquid was left between the ice. "Forget about her. I'll figure something out. Did you find out anything about Jade's case?"

"I didn't find a cell phone or tape recorder anywhere in the Inn." Jack Henry and I were sitting at table three in the restaurant. "I looked everywhere, then I got the call from Girl's Best Friend that my girlfriend was going nuts." His brows furrowed.

"I was just trying to save Artie from more heartache." I shrugged and scooped a spoonful of Granny's delicious brown beans out of the bowl before gobbling them down. I slathered some butter on a piece of Granny's fried corn bread and crumbled it up into the bowl.

"Emma Lee Raines!" Jade made me jump when she appeared next to me. "You have got to stop putting that junk into your body."

"I'll eat what I want." I stirred my spoon around the bowl, letting the corn bread soak up the bean juices.

"Emma." Jack Henry put his hands across the table and placed one on each of mine. "You are talking out loud again."

"She's driving me crazy about my food." I sucked in a deep breath.

"Hi, Emma and Jack." Tina Tuttle stood next to me, almost in Jade's ghost.

Jack and I nodded at her.

"Would you like to sit down?" Jack Henry asked Tina, and gestured to the empty seat.

"I'm sure you are busy." I couldn't believe he

just asked her to sit down. It was the only time we'd had together in the last twenty-four hours.

Of course she jumped at the offer and planted her butt in the chair, making me uncomfortable. She was as model perfect as Jade.

"I'd forgotten how pretty Sleepy Hollow is." She had a perfect seat facing the window that overlooked the mountainous area of our charming town.

"Where do you live again?" Jack asked. He eased back in his chair.

"I live in Canada now." She held her finger in the air to get Hettie's attention. "That's why I don't get back a lot."

"I didn't know you were working today," I said to Hettie. When Granny seated us and brought our order out, I figured she was manning the Inn on her own.

"I don't have a choice." Hettie glared at Tina. "After your friend canceled on me, I lost a full day of clients."

"She didn't pay beforehand?" I asked. Jade was beginning to leave a pattern at the shops around town. "Not that it's any of my business."

"No." Hettie shook her head. "I came over here to ask her about it, but her assistant wouldn't let me see her."

"What time was that?" Jack asked Hettie.

"Around seven-thirty, right?" Hettie looked at Tina. Tina shrugged. Hettie huffed, "I had transformed the entire studio into what she wanted and had all the food ready. It cost me a pretty penny, so I came over to get at least the food bill paid for."

All three of us watched as Jack Henry took out his notebook and wrote down what Hettie was telling us.

"Do you ever stop?" Tina laughed.

"Not during a murder investigation." He looked up at her.

"Good." Tina tapped the table with her fingernail. "Don't stop until you find out who killed my best friend. Which reminds me"—she leaned in and whispered—"did you check out Jade's assistant, Keisha?"

"She's on the list and while I was here I was hoping to ask her a few questions. Hettie, can I ask you a few questions?" He stood up when Hettie agreed. "Ladies, it's time I get back on the clock. If you'll excuse me." He walked over and kissed me on the top of my head.

Hettie excused herself as well and they walked out together.

"You are so lucky." Tina happily sighed. "Jack has really grown up. You can tell in his eyes that he loves you."

"He is sweet." I smiled, softening my walls I had put up against her. Even if she wasn't Jade, she was her best friend and it was hard for me to trust her.

"How on earth did you two get together?" she asked. Hettie brought her the iced tea she had ordered. "Is it sweet?" she asked.

"You did ask for sweet," Hettie said.

"Yes." Tina picked up the glass and took a long drink. There was satisfaction all over her face. "I do miss Zula's tea."

While she enjoyed her tea, I told her about how Jack and I started to date, leaving out the part where he caught me talking to my first Betweener client and how I helped him solve her murder.

"Jade was so jealous when we got back into town and found out the two of you were an item." Tina set the empty glass down. She lifted her hand in the air and tapped the glass when Hettie noticed her. "She'd die if she knew I was drinking this sweet tea." She laughed in remembrance. *"What are you thinking? That has a million calories in it and you are going to get fat,"* Tina said in her best Jade voice.

"Is she really making fun of me?" Jade's eyes narrowed, her mouth gaped open. "I can't believe she's making fun of me."

"I'm sorry you lost your friend." I wanted to acknowledge the loss. "I'm sure it's very hard."

"I can't imagine life without her. I mean . . ." Tina gulped. Tears settled on her eyelids. "She and I had lost contact when she got real big. I got married a year ago and sent an invitation to her agent. You couldn't imagine how happy I was on my wedding day when I saw her sitting in the church pew when I walked down the aisle."

Tina smiled. It was a warm smile.

"We talked every day since." She moved her hand and let Hettie set the glass down on the table. She picked it up and downed the entire glass of sweet tea. Tears dripped down her face.

"Tell her she was a wonderful best friend." Jade stood next to Tina and begged me to relay the message.

"I could tell Jade really cherished your friendship." I interpreted what Jade wanted me to say in my own words.

"I'm sorry, Emma Lee." Tina glanced at me. She bit her lower lip. Her hands trembled. "I'm sorry Jade was so mean to you when we were in high school."

"I'm sorry too, Emma." Jade nodded her head.

"It was her insecurities coming out in her. You were well liked by everyone and didn't have to put on all that makeup to hide the hurt like she did." Tina rambled on and on about how sorry she was for being mean.

"It's fine." I played off the real feelings I had. It wasn't like I was ever going to see Jade again once I helped her cross over. There was no reason for me to ever see Tina again either.

"I dropped off an outfit for Jade's funeral for Artie." Tina got up. She brushed the tears from her cheek. "I forgot the tiara I think she'd love to wear, but I'll bring it to the get-together tonight if that's okay."

"It's fine." I watched Tina leave the room before I got up to go to the kitchen to see Granny.

As I walked into the kitchen to say good-bye to Granny, I saw her and Jack Henry were sitting at the table. Granny was going over the events before she found Jade's body.

"There was no noise, no nothing." Granny's head slowly shook side to side. "She never complained about the service she got here."

"Is Keisha Ventord still here?" Jack asked.

"She is." She nodded. "She's gone on a cave exploration tour with Patricia and a couple of the cameramen. Sandford Brumfield took them along with another group of Inn guests."

Sandford was a tour guide and expert on all the caves our little town was known for. He had a sign-up sheet for his tours in the gathering room in the Inn for guests.

"They went on the flashlight tour last night."

Granny planted her hands on the table and pushed herself up to standing.

"What time was that?" Jack asked.

"Sandford picks everyone up around seven." Granny moseyed over to the counter and looked at the new food orders Hettie had stuck next to the stove.

"Seven, huh." Jack thumbed through his notebook.

"Are you sure, Granny?" I asked for good measure.

"As sure as I'm standing here breathing in this God-given air." She was offended I questioned her.

"Then that means none of Patricia, the cameramen, or Keisha could have killed her because the time of death doesn't match up." My idea of Keisha or Patricia killing Jade because she was mean to them and they had reached their tolerance level just fizzled out.

"So that leaves us with Marla Maria as the only one left who had a public fight with Jade." Jack tapped the notebook with the tip of his pen.

"I still want to talk to Beulah, so I'll go see her and Marla Maria while you go and finish up the autopsy reports with Vernon so I can get started on dressing Jade for her funeral." I got up from the table. On my way out I gave Jack and Granny a kiss 'bye.

I headed back to Eternal Slumber, where I found the paperwork Artie left with all the signatures I needed to start the funeral arrangements. I called Mary Anna to let her know it was official and confirmed that I'd see her in the morning.

"This is fast." The idea of her own funeral really seemed to bother Jade. "I mean he wants to get me in the ground super fast."

"I don't think that's it. I think he knows all of our classmates are in town and it would be a fantastic send-off for you if they could all be there." I ran my finger over the address Rolodex on my desk and stopped at the *K* for Kramer. I needed a horse for the carriage I had promised Artie. I'd worry about the horse now and the carriage later. Not that I had a lot of time.

"You need to find my killer." She stomped her pretty little high heel.

"One minute you want your murder to be solved, and the next you worry about your appearance." I had had it up to my chin with her as a Betweener client. "You have to help me by not disappearing on me."

"Who disappeared?" O'Dell Burns stood at my office door. He looked around my office to see whom I was talking to. Jade ghosted herself away like she had been seen.

"This piece of paper I have been looking for." I patted around my desk. "I should probably be more organized." I stood up. "What can I do for you, Mayor?"

O'Dell Burns was a snake in the grass. I'd steered clear of him since he and Granny had a fallin'-out. Truth be told, they'd had several fallin'-outs.

Burns Funeral Home had been my only competition until I saw Charlotte Rae kneeling down, practically on her knees, begging Artie for Jade's body. He and Granny fought over every dead person in this town. Even Granny's dead husband, Earl Way Payne. Earl Way hadn't changed his preneed arrangements once he and Granny tied the knot. When he died, Granny assumed he'd be laid out in the front window of Eternal Slumber, which is what she did. He looked mighty fine too, until the doors of the funeral home flew open and Ruthie Sue Payne, Earl's first wife, came in with O'Dell pushing the old church cart behind her. Right then and there, before God and all of Sleepy Hollow, O'Dell Burns grabbed up poor old Earl Way's dead body and carted him right on out of the funeral home and over to his.

Granny was mad as a wet hen when she saw that Earl hadn't changed his funeral arrangements.

When our last mayor had been carted off to jail, Sleepy Hollow had held an emergency election.

O'Dell Burns threw his name in the hat and when Granny got wind, she marched on down to the courthouse and put her name on the ballot. Never run a day in her life and knew nothing about politics.

"How hard can it be? Just a bunch of gossip and you know I'm pretty good at that," she had said, and winked.

Needless to say, Granny made it her life's mission to be a thorn in O'Dell Burns's side for the rest of her life. She swears it was why God blessed the earth with her presence. I said she's being ornery and mean. She'd say different.

"I wanted to congratulate you on securing the Peel girl for Eternal Slumber." He gestured his hand toward the chair in front of my desk.

"Yes. Please sit down." I eased into my chair. "Where are my manners?"

"I hear you left them back on the sidewalk in front of Girl's Best Friend." O'Dell snickered. "I'm sorry. Old habits."

After I took over Eternal Slumber when Granny retired, O'Dell Burns took out his revenge for Granny on me. He did everything in his power to one-up everything I did. Just like Charlotte Rae.

She'd turned into O'Dell Burns and it tore up my insides.

"I wanted to come see what you were thinking in terms of arrangements." He looked at his watch. "There are a lot of people angry that the reunion has been canceled. Not everyone was friends with Jade and they came here for the reunion."

"I'm going to follow her father's wishes and get the funeral ready for tomorrow afternoon." I shrugged. "It's just such bad manners to have a party when there has been a murder. I think we should go ahead and turn the reunion into a memorial. Food, dancing, seeing everyone and celebrating our class queen."

"Goody!" Jade reappeared. She bounced up and down on her toes. "That is a much better idea than a reunion."

It was just like Jade Peel to like anything that was just about her.

"That sounds like a very good idea. Sheriff Ross said he'd signed off on the body and was following some really good leads." Mayor Burns nodded. I was sure Jack told the mayor what he wanted to hear to keep him out of his hair. "How will you be able to tell everyone on such short notice?"

"I'll be sure to tell Beulah Paige. She'll spread the word like wildfire." I had intended to see her anyway since she had been with Jade yesterday when she rolled into town. Maybe she had a clue about something I didn't. "Plus I have Granny."

Both Mayor and I knew she was better than any newspaper article.

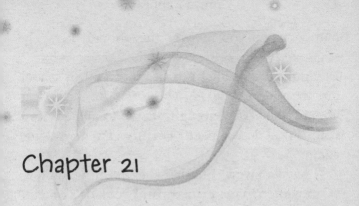

Chapter 21

Beulah Paige Bellefry lived clear on the other side of town in Triple Thorn subdivision. It was the fanciest subdivision in Sleepy Hollow. The next fanciest was the trailer park next to the cemetery on the back side of the town square.

Anyone who lived in Triple Thorn thought they were in high cotton, and they pretty much were right. And they let everyone know it.

On my drive over, I dropped off Jade's funeral cards at the printers and gave Granny a call.

"Sleepy Hollow Inn," she answered. "Zula Fae Raines Payne, proprietor, speaking. What can I do for you?"

"Granny, I don't think you need all that information when you answer the phone," I merely suggested.

"Emma Lee, I ain't got time for you to school me in manners when you seem to have lost yours." She wasn't going to listen to any advice I had. "What do you need? I'm busy. I'm here alone, again."

"I have a favor." I hoped she had time to do it. "Can you go to the printers and get Jade's funeral cards and pass them out at the town square?"

"Huh?" she asked.

"Artie Peel wants to have Jade's service tomorrow since everyone is in town for our class reunion and the *Sleepy Hollow News* doesn't print until next week, so I have no way of telling people." I knew Granny would tell the Auxiliary women and they'd help get the word out too. "Instead of canceling the reunion, I wanted to make it a memorial service."

"Sure, honey." Granny pepped up. "It could be good for the reality show."

"Granny, this is for a funeral. Do not make a spectacle of yourself or our town," I said, just as I pulled up to Beulah's driveway.

Granny harrumphed and hung up on me. Then I quickly dialed Dottie Kramer's number. She didn't answer, so I left a message on her machine about stopping by in an hour or so. More than likely, Dottie was home, but working out in her vegetable garden or flower beds.

Beulah's bright red Cadillac was parked in her driveway and the Dusting Dixies van was parked on the curb in front of the house.

"Good." I shut the engine off. "I can kill two birds with one stone."

I had been meaning to call Dixie Dunn, owner of Dusting Dixies, since my visit with O'Dell to let her know that we were still going to be needing her cleaning service at the school for Jade's impromptu memorial service.

I climbed the front porch and rang the doorbell. I stepped back and folded my hands in front of me.

"Emma Lee." Beulah tossed her red hair behind her shoulder. She wore a long cheetah-print silk shirt over a pair of black leggings and black flats. Her face was as tan as if she'd been to the beach for a week. Her lashes curled to the heavens and batted down to hell when she closed them. "Why on earth do you have any business being here? I told you last week I hadn't made my mind up about my demise."

It was her fancy way of telling me that she wasn't going to make any preneed funeral arrangements with me today. Recently I had been making my rounds throughout the community. Death was inevitable and no one wanted to hear about it.

"I'm not here for that." Over her shoulder I could see Dixie dusting the wooden staircase. "I'm here to let Dixie Dunn know that I will be needing her services after all."

That caught the ear of the town gossip queen.

"Why don't you come on in." Beulah couldn't resist a little afternoon gossip. "I was just about to have some tea."

She pulled the door wide-open and stepped back.

"I'd love to." I stepped inside.

"Emma." Dixie waved the feather duster in the air.

"Hi, Dixie." I waved back.

"Dixie, dear." I hated how Beulah talked down to Dixie. Dixie was older than her. "Emma has come by to let you know the reunion is still on. Isn't that right, Emma?" She looked at me for confirmation and then walked down the hallway into her kitchen.

"Actually, we are turning it into a memorial for Jade." I corrected Beulah. She was so good at assuming, but hey, it got me in the door. "I'm sure there will be a lot of people there so I wanted to know if you could help clean up afterward. And if I could hire you for the funeral tomorrow. Artie has asked for the service to be tomorrow afternoon at Eternal Slumber."

"I'll be there." She continued dusting up the banister and disappeared when she made it up to the top step.

"In here." Beulah passed me with a silver tray of whatnots to snack on and china teacups.

I followed her into the fancy sitting room. She placed the tray on the small coffee table. She took one of the cups and saucers off the tray, placing it in front of me.

My phone chirped twice. One message after the other. While Beulah busied herself with pouring the tea in the cups and making the treats look fancy, I read the messages.

The first one was from Shirley. She'd finally gotten back with me since this morning. She said she'd been busy cooking for the reunion and if it was canceled she'd use the food at Spare Time. I quickly texted back that I still wanted to use the food for tonight but instead of a reunion it was now going to be a memorial for our classmates to honor Jade. The second text was Jack Henry. He said that he still had no luck finding a car to match the description Jade had given in regard to the person from out front of the café the morning she got into town. He wanted to know what Artie had said or if I'd found anything else out from our little ghost friend.

"What on earth made Artie want to have the

funeral with you, and so soon?" She sat on the chair, crossed her ankles and held the saucer in her hands.

"I guess he likes Eternal Slumber." Was it so impossible for Beulah to think he'd laid Jade to rest with me?

"It wasn't like you and Jade were the best of friends." Beulah crossed her ankles, lifted her brows and let out a slight sigh before she took a sip of her tea.

"Plus all of our classmates are in town so it was a good idea to go ahead with the reunion but make it a memorial in honor of Jade. Vernon has pulled all the necessary evidence to release the body." I picked up the cup, holding it with both hands. The darn thing was so light and fragile, I was afraid of breaking it. "He asked my thoughts on having the funeral right away and Jade was so precious." The words were bitter in my mouth. I took a sip of tea to wash it down and continued, "Just so precious that I know she'd want the funeral as soon as possible and with her classmates by her side. I think she'd really have enjoyed a memorial in her honor too."

"My ass I do." Jade grunted from the arm of Beulah's chair. "I want you to stop running around town and figure out who killed me."

Beulah's eyes narrowed. "You don't have to pull

that good manners crap with me. Now I know you are putting me on."

"You are ignoring me." Jade walked over to the fireplace mantel and ran her hand down a crystal vase.

My hands shook. The teacup clinked as it rattled against the saucer. I tried to steady them. I tried to ignore Jade. She had been able to knock the tea glass out of my hand in the hearse, I could only imagine the scene if she knocked that vase off the mantel.

"Are you okay?" Beulah held the cup with her finger and thumb, curling her pinky out to the side.

"I'm fine," I said. "I just don't know why anyone would do such a thing. To think someone strangled her."

Beulah held her saucer in one hand. The other she used to massage her neck.

"I just can't imagine she'd have any enemies." I shrugged and took another sip of my tea.

"You don't think Beulah killed me, do you?" Jade ghosted herself next to Beulah. "I mean, I used to play with her pearls." Jade reached over and touched the strand around Beulah's neck.

"Well." Beulah put the saucer on the table and then touched her pearls. She did a little shimmy-shake and I could see goose bumps on her arms.

"I was one of the first people to talk to Jade when she came into town. I even had her and Tina Tittle over for tea yesterday afternoon."

"You did?" I put the saucer on the table and looked at Jade. It was a minor detail she'd left out. I leaned back into the couch and folded my arms.

"That camera crew was here. It was after she'd gotten her hair ruined by Mary Anna." She dragged her fingers through her hair. "Which reminds me that I need to get a new hairdresser."

"That was a big mistake on the manufacturer's part, not Mary Anna." I really didn't want to say anything about Artie and what he'd done. "In fact, Artie did ask Mary Anna to do Jade's hair for the funeral."

"Oh my God! I want Patricia to do it." Jade Lee stomped around like a bratty kid. I rolled my eyes. "And my tiara better be on my head too."

"Oh. In that case." Beulah let out a sigh of relief. "It's just so hard to find a good hairstylist." She looked off into the distance.

"What were you saying about the camera crew?" I asked, bringing her back to our conversation.

"Oh." She leaned over from her waist real far and whispered, "I went into the kitchen to get some more food because that Tina eats like a hog."

"She does. I told her she was going to blow up

like a balloon if she didn't stop eating so much."
Jade nodded.

"Jade didn't want them to film everything so I
fixed them their own plate of snacks in the kitchen
while we girls had our own little time together.
They talked about her like a dog and how stupid
she was. They even said that if she acted up one
time the producers were pulling the show."

"Pulling the show?" I gulped.

"Yes." Beulah eased back. She neatly folded
her hands in her lap. "I didn't tell no one because
when he noticed me looking at him with my
shocked face, he followed up with a 'just joking.'"

"Really?" I asked.

"That's not all." She leaned over again. "One of
the other cameramen laughed and said that there
was no way it was going to get canceled because
Jade was sleeping with the producer. And he's
married."

"No way." I shook my head. That bit of information was just like Hollywood gossip. "I couldn't
imagine her sleeping with a married man."

"You know what they say." She held her pinky
out to the side. Her ankles crossed. "Every dog
has a few fleas."

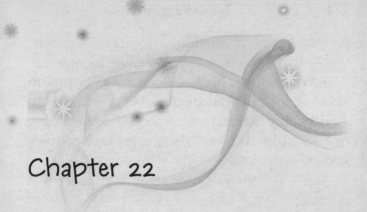

Chapter 22

"Why on earth didn't you tell me about going to Beulah's after your hair appointment?" I smacked the steering wheel of the hearse.

Jade had decided to join me and I was going to let her have it.

"I mean if you were having an affair and the cameraman knew, don't you think the wife would know." There were plenty of reasons for motives now. "Unfortunately, Granny said the cameramen and your people"—I referred to Patricia and Keisha—"went to explore the caves with Sandford, so we know all your people are clear."

I checked the time. Sandford lived across the street from Dottie Kramer, plus they'd started to date, maybe I could stop by his house to see what he had heard, if anything, from Jade's people. Surely they were back from the caves by now.

"I didn't tell you because I don't want anyone to know about it. It was one time." Little Miss High-And-Mighty had just been knocked down a rung or two off her ladder. "There is no way his wife knows."

"Jade . . ." My jaw dropped. "You aren't that dumb."

"I would know. My agent would've told me. Producers have loud mouths." Jade might be right. I had no idea how this whole Hollywood stuff was.

"Don't you think Jack Henry will get to the bottom of all this?" I asked. "If there was an affair, Jack will uncover it."

The hearse hugged the curves as I drove mock eighty. Jade gripped the door as if she feared for her life. I had news for her—she couldn't die twice.

"Where are we going?" she asked.

"I have to see Dottie Kramer about a horse and I want to talk to Sandford to see if your people said anything to anyone while they were bonding while kerplunking." I glanced over at her. Her tiara was starting to tarnish. "Are you okay?"

"I'm not sure." Her face was a wee bit whitish. "I'm starting to think that I'm never going to find peace. All of this is a bit overwhelming."

"So you do want to cross over?" I asked. She'd

been so wishy-washy about what she wanted in the afterlife.

She nodded. The tiara fell off into her lap. She looked at it.

"Even my tiara looks a little puny." A weak smile crossed her lips. "And I'd never stay in this kimono for more than a couple of hours, much less forty-eight hours."

"If you're ready, then you need to stick around and help me." This was a big turning point for my client.

"Here is what I know." She blew a couple of hot breaths on her tiara and rubbed it on her dress, trying to polish it. "I made the deal with the producer after our little . . . *ahem*." She cleared her throat and continued, "You know. I'm not very proud of it. In fact"—she harrumphed and stared out the window—"it was kinda like that casting couch call. We talked about the show, he invited me to have a drink in his office and the next thing I know, I woke up with my panties on the floor and he was asleep next to me." Her voice cracked. "The reality show contract was on the table with his signature. I'm not very proud of it."

"You think he slipped you something?" I asked. I had heard about those date rape drugs.

"More than likely. There's no way to prove it." She shrugged. "Anyways, I had been in rehab working on my self-esteem." She looked over at me. "Don't judge me."

"I'm not judging you. I'm trying to help you." I wanted to blurt out "Karma" because of how she treated me, but it wasn't necessary. "Trust me—if anyone had issues with their self-esteem, it was me. I mean, come on. I live in a funeral home." I made a joke and winked at her.

"I'm sorry for that. I know I told you before but I really mean that I am sorry for all the pain I caused you in high school." The ghost Jade was way nicer than the heart-beating Jade. "You have such natural beauty. Do you know how long it took me to get ready in the morning for school?"

"No clue." I didn't care either. I wanted to get to the details of her life up until someone strangled her, but if she felt this little confession was going to make her feel better, I would let her.

"Two hours." She laughed. "I swear, if I had to do it all over."

"You would?" I asked.

"Heck no!" She threw her head back and cackled so loud I couldn't help but laugh along with her. "Seriously, I've never met with the producer since. The details were left up to Mookie and him. I thought it was a great idea to come back to Sleepy Hollow for the first one. You know"— she lifted her hands in the air like what she was saying was in Broadway lights—"small town girl makes it big."

She blushed. I guess her hearing herself say those words to me embarrassed her a bit.

"It wasn't like I was going to really make fun of anyone." She glanced out the window. The scenery passed quickly by.

"You had a list of people to stay away from and you gave it to the cameraman," I told her what Keisha had told me.

"She has such a big mouth. I swear." Jade's lips pinched. Her eyes flinched a couple of times. "If I could fire her I would've a long time ago."

"Why? She seemed like she took good care of you." There was no way I would've let Jade talk to me like that even if the pay was good.

"She is a tattletale. She told Mookie everything. If Daddy hadn't confessed to sending Mookie the video of me when I went a little cuckoo outside of Girl's Best Friend, then I would've said Keisha had done it. She was always trying to sabotage me," Jade said.

"Like what?" I questioned, wondering if Keisha was the killer. Jealousy was a major player when it came to motive.

"She wanted to play a major part as my big assistant in the reality show and I don't, didn't, want to share the limelight. It was my idea and I wanted

it to be about me. You don't see other famous reality shows focus on the people behind the scenes."
Jade had a point.

"Did she ever threaten you?" I asked, hoping there was more to go on than just jealousy.

"No." She shook her head. "But I do know that she was the only one who knew about the affair."

"You mean you never told anyone?" I asked.

"Nope." Her voice was steady. "She was it. So I had no idea anyone knew about the affair until Beulah told you."

Now this was a piece of information I could use.

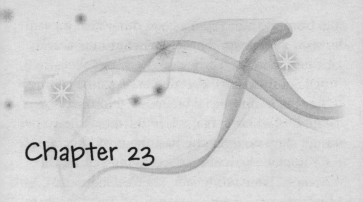

Chapter 23

S ome things never change." Jade nodded toward Dottie Kramer.

She was bent over jerking up carrots by their long leafy green tops. She always wore the exact same thing: a housecoat, hairnet and white nurse's shoes.

"That is what is so special about Sleepy Hollow." I wanted Jade to see the beauty around her. "Everyone has their own special quirk, but we all take care of each other. Look how this community turned out for you when you came to town. If there was a big red carpet to cover the town, they would've rolled it out."

"Mornin'." Dottie stood up when she heard me walking closer. She used her hand to shield her eyes from the sun. "Not a good day when the undertaker shows up." She let out a nervous laugh.

Undertakers and Jehovah Witnesses were two things Southerners didn't like to see come calling.

"I am here on official business." I looked down at her bushel of carrots. I could taste the juicy orange stick now. Dottie had the best vegetables in Kentucky. She made a good living selling them at Artie's. "I'm hosting Jade Lee Peel's funeral."

"Is that so?" Dottie asked, and went back to plucking up the carrots.

"And I was wanting to know if I could rent a horse from you." I watched as her hand curled around the carrot top and jerked up in one fluid motion.

"Daddy always said Dottie Kramer had a special touch and that was what made her vegetables so good." Jade strolled up and down the garden.

"Is that right?" Her face squished up as she tried to bring herself up to standing. She put her hands on her lower back and eased up more. "I'm getting too old for this. What does one of my horses have to do with Artie's girl?"

"Artie would like her to have a funeral fit for a princess. I was thinking along the lines of Cinderella and a carriage." I watched as Dottie picked up the bushel of fresh carrots.

"Well, come on." She gestured for me to follow her.

We headed to the small shed just a few yards away from the garden. Jade stayed in the garden looking at all of Dottie's hard labor. Something Jade knew nothing about.

Dottie put the basket on the wooden counter and handed me a knife.

"If you want one of my horses, you have to work for it." She opened and closed her hand several times. "I've got carpal tunnel and I'm having a hard time cutting off the carrot tops."

"I don't really have a lot of time." Was she serious? "I'll pay you to borrow a horse."

"I'm not interested in money. I've got plenty of it." She reached onto the floating shelf where there were some glass plates stacked high. She took a couple of the plates and laid them out in front of me. She opened a drawer and took out a bag of marbles.

Curious, I watched her and tried to cut off the carrot tops at the same time. She used the water pitcher and filled each plate with marbles and enough water in each plate to barely cover the tops of the glass balls.

She grabbed a handful of the chopped-off carrot tops and placed them cut side down on the marbles, going down the line.

"What are you doing?" I finally asked.

"This is how I have different types of carrots to

sell. I have the root kind." She pointed to the ones I was chopping. "When you remove the root, as you have done, it's not a taproot carrot that will regrow in a glass plate."

She opened up a mini refrigerator underneath the counter we were working on and pulled out two Ziploc baggies. She opened each of them and took out a carrot.

"Here, you can tell the difference." She popped one in her mouth. She closed her eyes and crunched down on the crispy vegetable.

I took one from each bag and took my time between them.

"They are good." I was surprised. I had seen the different packages in Artie's Meat and Deli, but never took the time to check out the difference.

"I've got just the horse for the funeral." Dottie had decided to let me off the hook and agree to the horse. "When do you need him, because I need to give him a good bath since my horses live in the pasture."

"Tomorrow afternoon around noon if that's good." I picked up another carrot and popped it in my mouth. The only thing I needed now was a Cinderella carriage. Where on earth was I going to find that? Charlotte Rae.

"Do you believe in the afterlife?" Dottie asked me the most peculiar question.

I gulped down the last bit of chewed carrot. I looked at Jade, who was still traipsing through the garden.

"Do I." I groaned, "More than you know." I sighed.

"According to Pastor Brown, our deeds on earth open the pearly gates." Dottie arranged the plates in the sunny part of the shed. "I'm worried for Artie that his little princess didn't make it to the pearly gates."

"Oh I'm sure she did." I knew she did.

"I'm not so sure. I saw how she treated people." Dottie never missed church and she took every word Pastor Brown spouted out from the pulpit for God's truth. "I was at the Buy-N-Fly getting some gas and them three girls were there. Artie's girl was giving some guy in a green car the business. He was getting gas and he said something to me about Jade thinking her you-know-what doesn't stink. I kept to myself. He said it loud enough for her to hear when she came out of the store. I told that boy not to let his mouth override his tail because she'd have the last word, but he didn't listen and I was right." She shook her head. "Poor guy didn't know what hit him."

"He was Jaded." My voice was almost an affront to silence. Everyone that had been Jaded had been a suspect in her murder.

"He was what?" Dottie asked.

"Nothing." I played it off. "Did you know the guy?"

"Not from here. He had plates from Ohio on an old Cutlass. Hadn't seen one of them in years." She grabbed the bushel basket. "Gotta keep going."

"What did they say to each other?" I asked, acting as if I was just prying.

"Her friends were in the Buy-N-Fly and she was running her mouth about his old car and how he was making her look bad when she rolled into town. He stepped away from his car and they had a fight between the pumps." Dottie shook her head. "He told her she was a selfish brat and that all she did was take up space and breathe good air. She was so mad. Then she smacked him."

"She what?" My jaw dropped. Shock and awe spread over me.

"Yep. The old flat palm across the face." Dottie laughed. "He reared up to come back at her but got his composure. He said he'd let her have it when she least expected it."

I followed her out of the shed. I needed to text Jack Henry. I didn't have much, but I did know that the guy was not from here. I had a state and a Cutlass. He could definitely put out an all-points bulletin, APB.

Chapter 24

After we left, I drove right across the street to see Sandford. Before we got out of the car, I called Jack Henry.

"Green Cutlass." I was sure Jack was writing down what I was saying because he had a habit of repeating me when he did to make sure he was hearing me right. "Older model."

"Jade had an affair with the producer of the reality show." It was an awful thing to tell him, but he needed to know all the facts.

"Oh my God, Emma! Why would you tell him that?" she cried from the passenger side. "That makes me look like a slut and I'm not."

"It doesn't make you look like a slut. If you want to help us bring your killer to justice, Jack Henry has to know the details too." Thank God the phone was up to my ear because Sandford was outside the fence feeding his goat herd and if I was talking to the air beside me, he'd call Granny just as fast as Doc Clyde had.

"She also said Keisha was the only one who knew it. I dropped by to see Beulah an hour or so ago and she told me that she overheard the cameraman telling the crew that Jade had an affair." I glanced over at Jade. She was gone.

"Who is the producer?" Jack asked.

"I would ask her, but she's gone." I was really getting sick of her not listening to me. "I told her that if she really wanted to find her killer, then she had to stay around and help me."

"At least you got me the Cutlass lead." Jack seemed happy with it. "Not that he is a suspect, but it's twice that he had a confrontation with her in public."

"Well, I'm at Sandford's and he's staring at me." I gave Sanford a slight wave when he walked toward the car. "I was at Dottie Kramer's getting a horse for Jade's funeral and I figured I'd stop over at Sandford's and see if he overheard any of Jade's people while he was taking them on the night tour."

"Good thinking." Jack sighed, "If you find out anything, do not go investigating. You tell me. Understand?"

"Got it." I heard him. After we said good-bye, I slipped my phone back in my pocket and got out of the car.

"Hey, Emma Lee." Sandford had a funny look on his face. The undertaker look was how I liked to refer to it. "What can I do you for?"

"I'm working on the eulogy for Jade Lee Peel and her assistant told me about them going on the flashlight tour the other night." A little white lie never hurt anyone. At least I told myself that. Though Granny would tell me that a lie was a lie no matter how big or small. Either way, I figured it was for the good of the community. I was helping get a murderer off the streets.

"Which one is her assistant?" he asked.

"Keisha. Big brown eyes. A little homely. Not the black-haired girl." Patricia and Keisha didn't look anything alike.

"She told you about the tour?" His troubled face looked like a graveled parking lot. "Because she didn't stick around. After I handed out the flashlights, she skedaddled."

"Long brown hair?" I placed my hand midway down my chest to show him the length of her hair. "Big eyes?"

He nodded. "Yep. That's her. I didn't catch her name." He shuffled his feet. "Some people can't do those night tours. It is real dark down there."

"Oh I know." I recalled the one-and-only time I'd gone down there and it was when my elementary school class went. I had nightmares for weeks and slept with a night-light for years after. "Do you remember what time that was?"

"I keep a journal log at the cave offices, but if I had to pull something off the top of my head, it's pretty much the same time every night. Around seven-ish."

"Seven-ish," I repeated.

If my calculations were right, it only took about fifteen minutes to get to the caves from town square and from the cave office it took another fifteen minutes, which meant that if Keisha had left, she had enough time to get back and kill Jade.

"Thanks, Sandford. Jack might be by to ask you some questions about that." I turned to get back into my car.

"How exactly are you going to use that in the eulogy?" he asked, bringing me back to my little white lie.

"It helps more than you know." I drew my lips into a tight smile, slamming the hearse door and drove off.

I pulled over to the side of the road and got out my phone.

"Hello," Jack answered.

"You have to find Keisha." My heart was beating a million miles a minute. "She went to the cave tour with Sandford, but left around seven-ish."

"Which means she really doesn't have an alibi with the group." Jack took a second to ponder the information I told him. "I'm almost at town now. I'll stop by the Inn and see her."

"Eternal Slumber!" Granny's voice came through the phone.

"What on earth is Zula Fae doing now?" Jack whimpered like a little puppy.

Sometimes Granny was just too much for all of us to handle.

I could still hear Granny screaming.

"What is going on?" I asked with trepidation.

"She's standing in the town square with some sort of hip-hop silk jogging suit on. Big pearls and a gold money symbol dangling around her neck. She has a megaphone she's screaming into. The camera crew is filming her." The quick bleep of a siren sounded. "And she's giving out some sort of pamphlet."

"Did you just flash your lights?" I asked, throwing the hearse in drive. The tires screeched when I peeled out.

The phone went dead.

Chapter 25

Eternal Slumber will take care of your family's needs. Your loved one will travel through space and time in a magical send-off. If Eternal Slumber is good enough for a big star like Jade Lee Peel, it's good enough for you!" Granny did a little two-step around the gazebo and screamed through the megaphone. She handed out the cards I had printed for Jade's funeral to the crowd that had gathered in front of the gazebo. "Did you get that?" She looked into the camera and gave a theatrical wink.

"Granny!" I screamed from the street and ran to the gazebo as fast as I could. "What are you doing?" I grabbed the megaphone out of her hands.

"I've gone and got me a YouTube channel and I've gone viral!" Granny looked surprised and somewhat thrilled at the reaction to her behavior. She turned to the cameraman, pulled her shoulders back and grinned.

"Who told you about YouTube?" I asked.

"Keisha." Granny's chin lifted up and then down. "She's a smart one. When I get this deal"—she pointed to the camera—"I'm going to hire her as my assistant since she's unemployed."

I did a long slow slide with my eyes and gave the cameraman the stink-eye. He dropped the camera to his side. I gave him the nod to move along. Jack Henry was busy ushering the crowd out of the town square by telling them that there was nothing to see.

"What are you doing?" Granny protested. "You asked me to spread the word about Jade's funeral."

"I did, but not dress up like some crazy old woman rapper and promote Eternal Slumber." My voice dropped when I saw a ghost-like thing off in the distance near Eternal Slumber.

Charlotte Rae's car was in the driveway. I was too busy paying attention to Granny when I pulled up and didn't even notice Charlotte's car.

"I'm telling you, I can get us a reality TV show and business for both of us will skyrocket." Granny wiggled her brows.

"No," I said with a tight voice. "You see where it got Jade Lee. I can't let this happen to you."

"You got things under control here?" Jack looked at me from under his brows. There wasn't happiness on his face.

"Understand?" I looked at Granny,

"Fine." Granny wasn't happy. Her beady eyes snapped at me a couple of times.

"Zula, is Keisha at the Inn?" Jack asked.

"Last time I checked she was. The crew informed me they would be leaving later today to catch a red-eye back to wherever they came from," Granny said.

"I'll walk you back over to the Inn. I have a few questions for her." Jack held out his elbow for Granny to take. No matter how much Granny frustrated us, she was as colorful as the beautiful backdrop behind the Inn.

I couldn't help but smile as I watched Jack in his brown sheriff's uniform and Granny in her bright jogging suit walking arm in arm across the square. So much love for both of them warmed my insides.

With a deep sigh, I turned around and looked at Eternal Slumber. As much as I didn't want to face Charlotte because I was upset with her, I couldn't wait to tell her that Artie commissioned me to host Jade's funeral.

Charlotte was exactly where I expected her to be when I walked in. Sitting in the chair next to the sideboard. Jade was sitting on top of it with her legs crossed, swinging the top one at Charlotte.

"I kept an eye on her just in case she tried something funny." Jade snarled and shook her fist at Charlotte.

"I guess congratulations are in order." Charlotte stood up. She tugged on the edges of her green jacket. Her eyes started at the bottom of my shoes and dragged to the top of my head. "You left out that little bit of information this morning."

Without her even saying a word, I knew she was judging my outfit. She was always on my case about wearing a suit on a daily basis, but that wasn't what I was comfortable with. And quite frankly, I think the community was more laid-back and appreciated how down-to-earth I was.

She put her hands together and clapped, slowly. She ran her hand down the sideboard.

"You know you really have messed things up for me." Her head twisted around. Her eyes were hard and cruel.

"I don't know what you are talking about. I never messed anything up." I rolled my eyes. I wasn't going to let Charlotte treat me like she deserved Artie's business.

"Don't you take anything from her. Besides"—

Jade stood next to Charlotte—"that shade is not her color. In fact, it makes her skin tone orange."

I didn't agree with Jade at all. I thought Charlotte looked amazing.

"The only thing that Artie liked that you said was about the carriage." I planted myself between her and the sideboard. "And this." I tapped the top of the piece of furniture. "Belongs to me. Would you like to sign the papers now?" I could see the stir of anger boiling in her eyes as I talked. My shoulders bounced up and then down when I let out a big huff. "If you'll excuse me, I've got to get on the phone and find me a Cinderella carriage unless you want to give me your contact."

"You haven't heard the last from me." Charlotte twisted toward the door, flinging her long curly red hair behind her shoulders. "I'll drag my feet on signing those papers too!"

"You will hear from my lawyer! And that green makes your skin look orange!" I blurted out like I knew something about fashion.

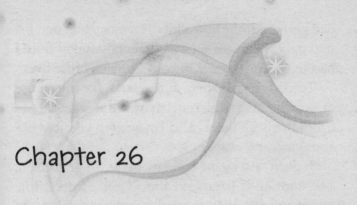

Chapter 26

N ow where are we off to?" Jade asked from the
front seat of the passenger side of the hearse.

"I've got about an hour to kill before I have to
come back and get ready for the reunion-turned-
memorial-service for you." I swear my blood pressure was still up from Charlotte Rae's little visit.
"I want to go and talk to Marla Maria about you."

"Why me?" Jade seemed offended.

"Because when she came to the Inn to ask you
to be a spokesperson for her pageant school, she
didn't seem very happy with you when you dis-
missed her."

Marla Maria's pageant school had been built on
Chicken Teater's piece of property on the outskirts
of town. It was her dream come true. From what I

had gathered, she had a lot of clients. I had no idea that pageants were such a big moneymaker until I had to go undercover to help Chicken cross over.

"I didn't dismiss her." Jade didn't like my choice of words. "No different than what you did to Charlotte back there. And I'm so glad you told her about looking orange."

"It didn't make me feel any better," I grumbled, and kept both hands on the wheel. "I don't like lowering myself to her level, but she makes me so mad when she thinks she's better than me. I wonder what she meant by I really messed up things for her."

When I thought about Charlotte's words, chills covered my entire body. There was some sort of warning in her voice. There was something bigger going on with Charlotte and I couldn't help but think it had to do with the Hardgrove's Legacy Center. My mind wandered to the big building and if the Hardgroves wanted her to secure Jade's funeral for promotional reasons like Granny had done in the square.

Regardless of what I thought, I had to put Charlotte in the back of my mind. My number one goal was to get Jade crossed over and then I'd deal with Charlotte.

"She deserves you to be nasty to her." Jade crossed her arms.

"Like Marla Maria, Mary Anna and Hettie deserved for you to be nasty to them?" It was okay for Jade to see the negative ways of other, but not herself. "You see where that got you."

"I'm not saying I'm proud of my behavior." Jade continued to stare out the front window. "I never asked anyone to kill me."

"Do you really think Keisha might've killed you?" I asked, wondering what her thoughts were.

"I don't think so." She brought her hands to her neck. She turned in the seat. She looked at me with shock and awe. "I do remember I was on the phone with Tina. I was telling her what I was going to wear to The Watering Hole and while I was talking to her, someone came up from behind me and wrapped the scarf around my neck." She gulped.

"Did you see them?" I asked. "Remember anything like hand size?"

She flung her hand in the air, flinging her fingers, trying to snap. "I'm going to learn to snap." She tried to no avail again. "The shoes!" Instead of snapping, she clapped. "They were the ugliest pair of shoes I'd ever seen. They were black and clumpy." Her face was a mask of unhappiness.

"Men's or women's?" It could be a good clue. I was still holding out hope for Jack to find the owner of the Cutlass. From how she treated him and from what Dottie said about their confrontation, he could be a very good suspect.

"I think." Her face contorted. "Crap, it's blank after that."

"At least it's something." I pulled into the Marla Maria's pageant school parking lot. I took out my phone and quickly texted Jack Henry what Jade had told me.

Jack Henry: *I'm going to have to meet you at the memorial. I'm still trying to find the Cutlass. The evidence is still building up against Fluggie. You and I both know she didn't do it. But . . .*

Me: *What happened with Keisha?*

Jack Henry: *Turned out she went to Pose and Relax and Girl's Best Friend. She collected the invoices for their services. Her alibi checks out. Hettie Bell even gave her a yoga class.*

Me: *Well, dang. Maybe the black shoes are a good clue. I'm going to see Marla Maria now just to make sure we mark her off the list.*

Jack Henry: *If you get any info, remember to tell me and not go off on your own.*

Me: *love you.*

Jack Henry: *love you too.*

"Aren't you two cute." Jade's voice dripped with sarcasm.

Marla Maria was sashaying the long, light, runway that spanned the length of the building. The heart-pounding music made the glass windows shake with each bass beat. There were a group of teenage girls at the back of the runway watching Marla strut her stuff.

When she saw me, she raised her hands, clapped them to the side. Like little robots, the teenage girls strutted the runway while Marla came over to me.

"If you want to be a pageant queen, you can forget it." She turned her nose up at me. "Those clothes." She ran her finger up and down my body. "I taught you better than that."

"Oh, hush," I laughed. "I wanted to ask you about Jade."

"Hmm." Her eyes narrowed. Her fake lashes drew down her cheeks. Her lips pinched.

"What exactly was your conversation with her at the Inn?" I asked.

"I told her who I was and how much I enjoyed watching her grow up since I too was a beauty queen in high school. I told her about my pageant school and wanted to know if she'd come by and meet with some of the girls." She pointed over to the runway. Jade was right up there with them. Only she was pretending there was a crowd and she waved to them, blowing air kisses to the pretend audience.

"These young ladies look up to people like Jade. They would've been thrilled to meet her." Marla continued, "She said she didn't have time and that she'd never heard of a pageant school. Then she walked off from me, dismissing me like trash."

"What were you doing that night around say . . ." I paused for good measure. "Seven-ish?"

"I have a full day of classes I teach. Every night at seven I have my ten-year-olds." She put her hand on her hip and cocked her leg out. "Why are you asking me this, Emma Lee?"

"I'm doing her eulogy for her funeral tomorrow and I'm having a hard time finding anything positive to write about her," I lied, yet again.

Marla didn't need to know that I was trying to help Jack Henry so I could help myself get Jade to the other side. I would tell Jack what I'd found out and that she had an alibi. If he needed to check it out, it should be easy to do so.

My phone vibrated in my pocket. It was Fluggie. I'd yet to hear from her all day.

"I've got to take this." I waved 'bye to Marla Maria. She waved 'bye to me and joined the girls on the runaway. "Hey, Fluggie."

"Have you gotten any news?" she asked.

"No. Just that the car from Jade's confrontation was a guy driving a green old model Cutlass. Everyone seems to have alibis." I got in the hearse and hooked my phone up to my earbuds. "Keisha was at a yoga session at Pose and Relax with Hettie." There was no need to go into detail since she and Hettie were cleared. "Patricia and the camera crew were with Sandford on a night cave tour. Mary Anna was at bingo. Marla Maria was teaching ten-year-olds how to be pageant winners. Tina Tittle was on the phone with Jade when she died."

That about summed up everyone that Jade had hung around or Jaded.

"Did Jack find my phone or another phone?" Fluggie asked.

"Not that I know of, why?" I asked.

"Because there was no phone call from Tina Tittle on the phone I picked up. Only business calls." Fluggie caught me again. "Did Tina say that?"

Crap, crap, crap.

"Jack Henry said something about it." It wasn't like I could say that Jade recalled the exact moment she was killed. I lied again, "There was some evidence collected about a pair of men's black shoes. So I really wonder if the guy in the Cutlass is the one."

"Well, I need to find him because my attorney called and he said that my DNA was all over Jade's room along with hers. No one else's and they do have sufficient evidence to charge me." Fluggie sounded desperate. "I'm the only person that doesn't have a witness to me being at the old mill around seven when I grabbed all my equipment so I could take photos at The Watering Hole. I swear I won't sleep until I find that killer."

"I'm sure we will figure it out," I assured her, though I felt like we were running out of time. I could tell by Jack's text and my gut.

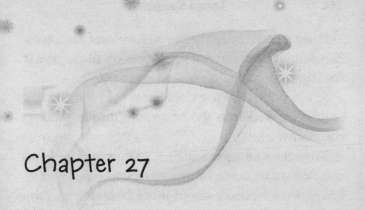

Chapter 27

W hat on earth am I going to wear?" I went
   through my closet. What I had planned to
wear was definitely not appropriate anymore. The
strapless red dress and red heels were more for a
party, not a memorial.

"Are you asking for my expertise?" Jade stood
in my bedroom.

"I guess you liked the pageant school?" I asked
because she hadn't left with me.

"That Marla Maria is a genius. If I was living,
I'd so open me up a chain of pageant schools." She
walked over to my closet. "You can still wear the
red dress."

"I don't know." It was a stretch for me to wear
to the reunion.

"I do. And I want everyone to look fabulous. Not sad, grumpy or frumpy." She winked. "Wear the dress."

I pulled it out of the closet and held it up to my chin. I walked into the bathroom and looked in the mirror.

"You do look good in red." She stood behind me. Both of us stared at my reflection. "But you've got to do something about those panties."

"You don't need to worry about my panties," I warned. "And if Jack comes back here tonight, you scatter."

Jade disappeared while I finished getting ready. I wasn't surprised she didn't ride with me in the hearse to the memorial. There was no way in life Jade would arrive to an event, even her own memorial, in a hearse, much less in death.

The memorial was packed. There were even people there from the community that hadn't gone to school with us, along with the camera crew.

"Emma!" Jade screamed above the DJ's music. She was in the middle of the school gym standing behind a circle of people. She was pointing to the middle with one hand and waving me over with the other.

"Hey there." Cheryl Lynne touched my arm and handed me one of the two glasses of wine she was holding. "This turned out really nice. You really outdid yourself for someone that you were fuming about just a day ago."

"I know. I feel bad for Artie and really I never wished anything bad to happen to her." It was sad that I had gotten to know Jade in death better than I had in real life. The truth was that death changed her attitude, which was a lesson all the living could learn. "From now on, I'm going to try to be a nicer person to everyone. Even if they aren't nice to me."

"I don't think you ever had to worry about that. Everyone likes you." Cheryl waved to someone in the distance. "Look, it's Daryl Davis."

"Who?" I asked.

"Shh." She ran her hands through her hair. "He's coming over."

"Ladies, ladies, ladies." Daryl Davis, someone I didn't remember, walked up with a silk brown shirt tucked deep into a pair of black slacks. His shirt had three buttons unbuttoned and a few black hairs stuck out from underneath. He ran his hands over his heavily gelled black hair, sniffed and grabbed Cheryl. "You look amazing."

"Oh, Daryl." She blushed, pushing him off her. "You were always a charmer. Wasn't he, Emma Lee?"

"Mmm-hmm." I pinched a forced smile. I looked over Mr. Sauvés's shoulder to see Jade jumping up and down in the middle of the crowd pumping her arm up and down in the air.

"What can I say?" He winked, giving me the creeps. Seriously, he was one gold chain away from a small role on *The Sopranos*.

"Hey, sexy." Jack Henry's arms came around me from behind. His words hot against my ear.

"Jack." I turned around and found my handsome other half looking all cleaned up in slim-fitting gray suit pants and jacket. He had a black button-up shirt on underneath. "You look . . ."

"Delicious." Jade purred like a kitten next to me. "Emma Lee Raines. I hope you didn't wear those granny panties."

"She's here?" he asked.

I nodded.

"Who's here?" Daryl pushed between us with his hand held out. "Jack Henry Ross. Dude, you look even better as a grown-up. Man, how are you?"

"Davis!" Jack obviously remembered this meathead. "I'm great. How are you?"

"Better than I deserve." Daryl's lips did that duck bill thing and he slowly nodded. "Single." He elbowed Cheryl. "Maybe not for long. Own my own real estate company up in Lexington and I have my own hot tub."

"You do." Jack tried to act impressed, but I knew better.

"Yep. It's outside on a deck I built around it." He whipped out his phone and swiped his finger across the screen as he showed us his photos.

I couldn't help but look.

"Wait," I protested when I saw something that was green.

"What?" Daryl snarled.

"Can you go back?" I gestured with my finger over top of his phone. "I think I saw something neat."

"Sure." His ego inflated with each swipe of his finger.

"There." I pointed and looked up at Jack's face when he noticed it was a green car.

"My girl." He grinned so big. "Calli."

"Dude, that's a great car." Jack played along. "Tell me about it."

"I don't have to tell you about Calli the Cutlass." Daryl stuck his phone back in his pocket. "I can show you."

"Great. Now?" Jack asked a little too enthusiastically. I glared between the two of them.

I wanted so badly to point at him and blurt out, "Murderer!" But I knew I couldn't.

"You." Jade gasped when she saw Daryl. "Well if this just takes the cake."

My jaw tensed. My eyes fluttered between ghost Jade and Daryl.

"I ought to give you down the road!" She shook her fist at him. "If I weren't a lady and beauty queen, I'd . . ."

She hollered and fussed and flew off the handle—only he couldn't hear her. I could and I was taking it all in.

Jack looked at me, giving me the look that asked me if my Betweener client was here. I slowly nodded.

"Going nuts," I mouthed, hoping he could read my lips.

"Well, let's go take a look because we are burnin' daylight." Jack smacked Daryl's back. To make it look sincere, Jack leaned in and acted like he was going to kiss me. He whispered, "Act like we are saying a long good-bye. Is she here?"

I pulled him to me and looked over his shoulder, scanning the room. She was gone.

"I don't see her and she was just right here cussing him out." Was it true? Was Daryl Davis the killer? My insides felt like there was electricity running through me or I'd had too much coffee from Higher Grounds. I gripped Jack's back.

"Call the department and tell them about the car. Send a deputy," Jack whispered in my ear and put his hand on the back of my head. He kissed my cheek.

When he pulled away from me, our eyes held for a few seconds.

"You are whipped, man." The back of Daryl's hand smacked Jack's bicep.

"Let's go see that car." Jack and Daryl walked off.

"Isn't he something?" Cheryl was grinning from ear to ear.

"He's definitely something all right." I groaned, bringing the wineglass up to my lips. "I need to make a call."

"Fine." Cheryl started to bebop toward the group of people who were in the middle dancing.

I slipped out into the hall and called dispatch like Jack told me to do. Any minute some backup would be here to help him. Hopefully he was out there checking out the car and making Daryl think he was really interested.

Nervously I gulped down the wine and on my way over to the bar, the sound system squeaked. I stopped and looked up at the gym stage.

"I would like to thank everyone for coming." Artie's hand gripped the microphone. "Jade would have loved this reunion. She would've told us to go on as planned, but she would've also wanted to be memorialized," he joked. The crowd laughed. "You know that she loved a good party and enjoyed being center of attention. It's my fault. I did make her the center of my life. She had a hard time when her mother passed away and I made sure she was pampered and taken care of. I know that she is reunited with her mother. I can't help but ask that if anyone knows anything about her murder, please come forward with any information. Sheriff Ross, your own classmate, is here tonight and please give him any tips you might have. Even if they don't seem to be a big tip, any tip is big." He pulled something from his pocket. "I'm going to offer a ten-thousand-dollar reward in the case." He held a check above his head.

Any minute I was sure Jack would be in here and let Artie know that he could keep his money. There was a murmured wave over the crowd. Anyone in Sleepy Hollow would go nuts if they won ten thousand dollars. It didn't matter how much the Powerball jackpot was every week, the Buy-N-Fly was always packed on Friday nights with lottery winner hopefuls.

Cheryl Lynne was back by the bar yakking it up with someone I didn't recognize and the DJ was still playing the tunes. Jade did love a great party.

I glanced up to the ceiling picturing Jade sashaying down the gold road she'd told me about.

"There you are." Jack Henry brought me out of my dream.

"How did it go?" I asked.

He grabbed my hand and dragged me out of the gym.

"Where are we going?" I asked when we crossed the tape the school janitor had put up to hinder any stray memorial visitors from roaming around the school.

"I've always wanted to make out in the locker room." Jack Henry pulled me into the doorway when we turned the corner. "I think we got our murderer and we can get on with our night."

"No alibi?" I asked.

"None with anyone that can corroborate his story." Jack pulled me closer. "He admitted being disgusted with her on the two occasions. In front of the café and then at the Buy-N-Fly. He said he was going to embarrass her at the reunion and that was what he meant when he said he was going to get her back. We've got people interrogating him now."

His lips seared a path down my neck.

"Jack," I whispered, and looked down the hallway. "You are being bad."

I joked, kind of liking this spontaneous Jack Henry Ross.

He took my lips in a soft moist kiss. My body melted against his. The pressure of his lips increased. His hands ran down the sides of my arms and his fingertips found the hem of my skirt. His fingers grazed my leg, sending chills all over me as they moved up my thigh.

"I could never get him to do this with me." Jade leaned up against the wall in the hallway.

"Go away," I gasped. "I warned you."

"Huh?" Jack Henry pulled away.

"No." I grabbed him by the shirt and brought him closer. "Not you. Her."

Jack looked over my shoulder.

"You mean her as in Jade?" His lip cocked. "You mean Daryl Davis isn't her killer?"

My heart sank. Jack ran his hands through his hair.

"This case is never going to get solved." Jack was frustrated. "I thought we had him."

I held up one finger. "You wait right here. I'm going to go have a talk with her in the bathroom."

"I'm going to have to go back to work and somehow let Daryl go." Jack chewed on the inside of his cheek. "I don't have time to wait."

He kissed me good-bye and walked down the hall the opposite way.

I stalked down the hall with Jade by my side.

"I'm glad you want to talk to me because the first thing you need to do when we get into the bathroom is get rid of those big granny panties." She snarled from behind me.

"You just ruined it." I threw my hands up in the air. "Daryl Davis obviously didn't kill you because you are still here. Jack had to go to the station to somehow clear him."

I opened the door to the bathroom.

"Thank you so much." Tina Tittle stood in front of the mirror with a tiara on top of her head. Her purse was laid open in the sink. A pair of black men's shoes were sticking out of her purse. There was a phone propped up on the back of the sink. "Emma."

She jumped around. She grabbed the tiara off her head and stuck it in her purse. She grabbed the cell.

"You scared me." She smiled and let out a deep sigh.

"That's my phone!" Jade rushed over to Tina. "I have that purple case on my phone. Why does she have my personal phone?" I looked at her. "What? I have a business phone and I have a personal phone." She pointed to the shoes. "Those are the shoes the killer was wearing."

"Why do you have Jade's phone?" I asked. Then it hit me. "Oh my God." My mouth dropped. "Tina, you didn't."

"Jesus, Emma." She let out another big huff before pulling out the tiara and a gun. "You always have stuck your nose into other people's business just like your granny."

I glared at her. Anyone that talked about my granny set me on fire. She pointed her gun at me.

"Jade was your best friend." I was beginning to get dizzy. I gripped the trash can next to me to help steady myself.

"Is the creepy funeral home girl getting scared because she's afraid her sister is going to host her funeral?" Tina talked with duck-billed lips in a whiny voice. "I about died when Artie decided to let you, of all people, host Jade's funeral. She hated you."

"No I didn't." Jade was quick to come to my defense. Too bad she was dead and it looked like I was going to join her any minute.

"She still didn't deserve to die." I took a deep breath. I had to get out of there.

"She did have to die," Tina said with a flat voice. "She did deserve it."

She shooed me into one of the bathroom stalls. She kept the door open with her hip.

"Sit down," she ordered. "Why on earth did you have to come in here? I hate to have to kill you because I was almost home free."

"Why did you do it?" I had to know before she killed me. The entire thing had stumped me.

"Jade had nothing to do with me after high school. She divorced our friendship. Something about having to let her past go if she was going to find her future. She found out that I was marrying a producer of reality shows and immediately came to see me. I thought she was really there to rekindle our friendship. The only thing she kindled was my husband loins." She pulled out Jade's phone. She swiped her fingers over the screen and showed me a picture of Jade and a man in a very compromising position. "That's her, on my husband. Then she gets the reality show."

"That's a good reason to kill her." I couldn't help but say it.

"I told her how he drugged me." Jade stomped around the bathroom. "How can I get help to you? I never thought she was the one who killed me. I was on the phone with her when I got attacked."

"He drugged her though," I spouted.

"Did she tell you that?" Tina seethed. "Who else did she tell?" She jabbed her gun my way.

"No one." This was not the time to forget my conversations with my ghosts. "She said how much she loved you and was glad that your friendship withstood the hardships. She was so proud of your bond with each other."

"No she wasn't. Did she tell you that? Because when I was on the phone with her, she said that she was going to expose my husband drugging her because he canceled her little show before it even got the first episode filmed." She glared.

Things were becoming very clear to me.

"You mean to tell me that after Jade found out the show was canceled, she called you and that was when the threats started?" I asked. Tina nodded. "You showed up at her room at the Inn and killed her."

"Better than that." She grinned, pleased with her actions. "I was standing outside her room when I called her because I knew if the police did track her calls from the phone carrier, that it would show I had just gotten off the phone with her and there was no way I killed her."

"You had a reason to kill her. She was going to blackmail you. The police will understand."

I did my best to talk myself out of the mess I'd gotten into.

"Emma, honey." She threw her head back in a fit of laughter. "I'm not stupid. My husband is the producer of those cop shows. They will throw me in jail forever. It was perfect, though Vernon Baxter was pretty good with figuring out the strangling. I thought for sure I'd made it look like a suicide since she was so crazy and had the nut house records to prove it."

"I'm not crazy!" Jade fumed. "I'm a beauty queen! Take my tiara off now!"

"How did you get Daryl Davis's shoes?" I asked.

"Poor Daryl. He was insurance for my freedom,

but it looks like you've screwed that up. Daryl is sitting in jail while you are being killed, which doesn't make him your killer, so maybe I'll make you strangle yourself." She waved the gun in the air. "Have you ever contemplated suicide, Emma Lee Raines?"

I kept my mouth shut.

"Anyways, Daryl was so mad at Jade that he even threatened her. While they were busy cussing each other out at the Buy-N-Fly, I took his shoes out of his car without him looking. I made sure I wore them to the Inn just in case my plan didn't work out and Jade noticed the shoes. She would notice something as stupid as a pair of shoes." She was still waving that gun around. "She was so shallow. She always judged people by their shoes. She was wrong this time."

"Well I'll be." Jade stood behind Tina, snapping away. "I can snap." Jade smiled. She looked up at me. Then she looked over my shoulder. Her eyes glistened.

I looked behind me at the wall. I was seeing the old orange tile that had been there since I was in high school.

"Do you see that?" Jade asked. I turned back and looked at her over Tina's shoulder. "It's beautiful," she whispered. "Emma, I think I'm ready to go to the big pageant in the sky."

I watched Jade sashay past me, swinging her hips and snapping her fingers until she was gone.

"What are you looking at?" Tina asked, bringing me back to the living.

Just as she turned around, the trash can came barreling out of the air, knocking Tina Tittle in the head and out cold.

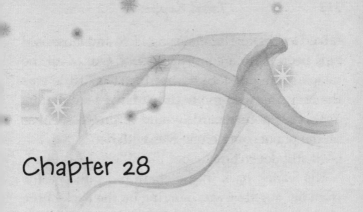

Chapter 28

"How did you figure it out?" Jack Henry asked Fluggie Callahan.

After Fluggie knocked Tina out, I was too stunned to do anything, so I sat there while she called the Sleepy Hollow Police.

Tina didn't even come to when they put handcuffs on her. For good measure, they took her to the hospital to see if she had gotten a concussion, but not without the police guarding her room.

"I know you are going to get mad, but Emma Lee and I have done some sleuthing on our own." Fluggie thought she was telling Jack something he didn't know. "We had crossed off suspects one by one. When you hauled off Daryl Davis for questioning, I knew he wasn't the killer because I had talked to him at The Watering Hole and Hoss said he'd been there a couple of hours. Out of all the people who Jade let into her life, Tina Tittle was the only one who really didn't have a solid alibi. Yeah, the phone records would've shown she was on the phone, but no one was with her."

"It still doesn't make her the killer," Jack noted.

She leaned back in the chair and pulled a file from her bag that was hanging on the back of the chair. She threw it on the desk. Jack opened it up and took out some photos.

"I went to the library earlier in the day and looked up all of Jade's friends from high school. These are all the photos the library had and the school yearbooks. Tina is in almost all of them. She is looking at Jade with that jealous look on her face any woman would recognize. That was my first clue."

Jack looked carefully at each picture.

"The camera crew's red-eye was delayed due to Mother Nature's downpour when the fog rolled in so they came to the memorial to get some footage like the rest of the news crews. Being a reporter, I notice a lot of things." Fluggie tooted her own horn. "The camera equipment is stamped with a Canadian airlines logo. I recalled Tina saying something about being from Canada. I did a little Google search." She put her hands out in front of her like she was typing. "With a little snooping, I found that Tina's husband is the producer and the man Jade had the affair with. What more motive do you need to kill someone?"

"You were right." Jack put the pictures back in the file. He closed it and handed it back to her. He looked at me. "Are you okay?"

"Much better now that Fluggie saved me." I patted my friend sitting next to me.

"Now you really owe me." Fluggie stood up. She grabbed her bag. "I've got to go. I'm putting out a special edition of the *Sleepy Hollow News* in the morning. I'll be sure to add Jade's funeral arrangements."

Jack had to finish up some paperwork, but he promised me he would come stay the night since we barely had any time together.

Eternal Slumber was completely dark when I opened the front door. I flipped on the light switch next to the door.

"Charlotte Rae!" I jumped when the light illuminated my sister sitting in the chair next to the sideboard.

Her pink suit had a little dirt on the front and the curls of her hair were falling flat.

"You scared the crap out of me. What is wrong with you?" I asked.

"Nothing." She looked sad. "I told you that your actions would have consequences."

"Whatever. I don't even know what that means."
I planted my hands on my hips. "It's late and I just
almost got killed. So if you wanted to come here
and bully me, you can just leave. I'm tired and I
want some sleep."

I walked over to the door and opened it wide,
giving her the unspoken signal to leave.

Gracefully she got up and walked out the door.

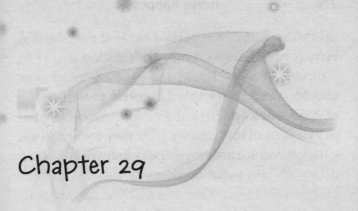

Chapter 29

The sun streamed through the window. I rolled over and looked at Jack Henry. He must've slipped in without me hearing him because I never woke up. He was in a deep sleep, his heavy breathing was the clue.

I eased myself out of bed and looked at the clock.

Jade's funeral was today and I hadn't heard from anyone I had contacted about a carriage for Dottie's horse to pull Jade's casket around the square and to the graveyard.

I tiptoed out of the room so Jack could sleep a little longer and made my way down to the kitchen to get a cup of coffee. The basement rattled with movement. I looked out the window and saw Mary Anna's car parked in the drive. She was busy getting Jade ready for her final debut.

"Hey, Granny." I held the phone between my shoulder and ear while I poured myself a cup of coffee and added some cream. "Do you want to run up to Hardgrove's with me? I want to get Charlotte to sign those papers and maybe she'll do it with you standing there."

"I reckon I can," Granny said. The rattling pans clinked behind her. "I got Hettie here fixing some of them crazy healthy snacks for the snack room, so the Inn will be fine in her hands. I'll be right over."

Without waking up Jack, I pulled on a pair of jeans and T-shirt and brushed my hair so it wasn't sticking up all over. When I heard the whiz of the moped shut off and the sound of a heavy chain, I knew Granny had parked her moped by the big Oak tree in front and locked it up tight.

Unfortunately, our trip was a bust. Charlotte was too busy showing off her fancy new job to even listen to anything I had to say. But the best part was how one of her customers made no qualms about how unhappy they were with how Charlotte had handled her event.

I was too spittin' mad to even talk about Charlotte Rae. And I just couldn't understand why she wouldn't sign the papers turning the funeral home over to me like she was supposed to do.

In no time and a little bit of a lead foot, I had the hearse parked in the back of Eternal Slumber. It was still strange not seeing Charlotte's car parked in the space right up against the back door, because Lord forbid she walk any further than she needed to. Charlotte always claimed that since she was the one who "sold" our packages that she needed to be presentable, which meant the less she did to mess herself up the better.

While Charlotte was here, I was in charge of making sure the arrangements for the family were carried out as they had planned, the burial service was ready, and all the details were taken care of, like the repass, flowers, memory cards, and any other details.

"I better get out of here." Granny opened the door and grabbed her black leather touring helmet off the seat next to her and strapped it under her chin. "I left Hettie in charge and God only knows what concoction she made at the juice bar. Plus I still have to make my pies for dinner tonight."

With Granny on her way, I finished up the touches of Jade's funeral by getting the chairs set up and making sure Vernon, Mary Anna, and Jack were ready with their parts of the service.

In fact, I had just enough time to make one last-ditch effort to get Charlotte to sign the papers, so I zoomed back out of town to no avail. Charlotte and Gina Marie Hardgrove were in a heated discussion on something Charlotte had messed up and she just shoo'ed me off. But happy to see that there was a carriage hooked up to Dottie's horse in the front yard of Eternal Slumber. Someone must've gotten my message.

Within a couple of hours, Charlotte had come to Eternal Slumber to pay her respects to Jade's father but didn't want anyone else to see her so she hid in the office and waited for me because she wanted to talk to me. No doubt about the contract.

While I stood next to Granny greeting mourners a cackle from the vestibule caught my attention as Granny walked over to me to stand in the back.

"What is Charlotte doing?" I groaned and gave my sister the stink eye when I realized it was her laughing. She took a seat next to the sideboard table. "She told me she didn't want anyone to know she was here. And now she's making fun of the sound system."

"Hi-do," Granny nodded at a couple of late folks as they walked by and took a seat in the back of the viewing room. "Where is she?"

"By the sideboard," I bent over and whispered. Charlotte smiled her pretty smile, crossed her long, lean legs and twiddled her fingers in the air at me, giving me a little wink. A wink in Sleepy Hollow said more than a thousand words. "Uh." I glared at her. "Of course she didn't mean it. She wants everyone to see her," I whispered.

"Where?" Granny asked again. Her eyes darted around the vestibule.

"In the chair." I pointed to Charlotte in the chair. "Oh." My mind reeled. "If she thinks she's going to sit there by that sideboard after I told her that she couldn't have it, she's got another thing coming to her." I wagged my finger at Charlotte.

Granny smacked my hand.

"Emma Lee Raines, that chair is empty." Granny put her hand up on my forehead. "Are you getting sick? Have you taken your meds?"

"So you really can see dead people?" Charlotte Rae was suddenly next to me. "And you really don't have the 'Funeral Trauma'?"

Suddenly things had become very clear.

Charlotte Rae Raines wasn't there to visit her family home, make amends with me, sign the papers or help me with Jade Lee Peel's funeral. She was there as a Betweener client.

A GHOSTLY UNDERTAKING

**A funeral, a ghost, a murder . . . It's all in a
day's work for Emma Lee Raines. . . .**

Bopped on the head from a falling plastic Santa,
local undertaker Emma Lee Raines is told she's
suffering from "funeral trauma." It's trauma all
right, because the not-so-dearly departed keep
talking to her. Take Ruthie Sue Payne—innkeeper,
gossip queen, and arch-nemesis of Emma Lee's
granny—she's adamant that she didn't just fall
down those stairs. She was pushed.

Ruthie has no idea who wanted her pushing
up daisies. All she knows is that she can't cross
over until the matter is laid to eternal rest. In the
land of the living, Emma Lee's high-school crush,
Sheriff Jack Henry Ross, isn't ready to rule out
foul play. Granny Raines, the widow of Ruthie's
ex-husband and co-owner of the Sleepy Hollow
Inn, is the prime suspect. Now Emma Lee is stuck
playing detective or risk being haunted forever.

Another day. Another funeral. Another ghost.
Great. As if people didn't think I was freaky enough. But, truthfully, this was becoming a common occurrence for me as the director of Eternal Slumber Funeral Home.

Well, the funeral thing was common.

The ghost thing . . . that was new, making Sleepy Hollow anything *but* sleepy.

"What is *she* doing here?" A ghostly Ruthie Sue Payne stood next to me in the back of her own funeral, looking at the long line of Sleepy Hollow's residents that had come to pay tribute to her life. "I couldn't stand her while I was living, much less dead."

Ruthie, the local innkeeper, busybody and my

granny's arch-nemesis, had died two days ago after a fall down the stairs of her inn.

I hummed along to the tune of "Blessed Assurance," which was piping through the sound system, to try and drown out Ruthie's voice as I picked at baby's breath in the pure white blossom funeral spray sitting on the marble-top pedestal table next to the casket. The more she talked, the louder I hummed and rearranged the flowers, gaining stares and whispers of the mourners in the viewing room.

I was getting used to those stares.

"No matter how much you ignore me, I know you can hear and see me." Ruthie rested her head on my shoulder, causing me to nearly jump out of my skin. "If I'd known you were a light seeker, I probably would've been a little nicer to you while I was living."

I doubted that. Ruthie Sue Payne hadn't been the nicest lady in Sleepy Hollow, Kentucky. True to her name, she was a pain. Ruthie had been the president and CEO of the gossip mill. It didn't matter if the gossip was true or not, she told it.

Plus, she didn't care much for my family. Especially not after my granny married Ruthie's ex-husband, Earl. And *especially* not after Earl died and left Granny his half of the inn he and Ruthie had owned together . . . the inn where Granny and Ruthie both lived. The inn where Ruthie had died.

I glared at her. Well, technically I glared at Pastor Brown, because he was standing next to me and he obviously couldn't see Ruthie standing between us. Honestly, I wasn't sure there was a ghost between us, either. It had been suggested that the visions I had of dead people were hallucinations . . .

I kept telling myself that I was hallucinating, because it seemed a lot better than the alternative—I could see ghosts, talk to ghosts, be touched by ghosts.

"Are you okay, Emma Lee?" Pastor Brown laid a hand on my forearm. The sleeve on his brown pin-striped suit coat was a little too small, hitting above his wrist bone, exposing a tarnished metal watch. His razor-sharp blue eyes made his coal-black greasy comb-over stand out.

"Yes." I lied. "I'm fine." Fine as a girl who was having a ghostly hallucination could be.

"Are you sure?" Pastor Brown wasn't the only one concerned. The entire town of Sleepy Hollow had been worried about my well-being since my run-in with Santa Claus.

No, the spirit of Santa Claus hadn't visited me. *Yet*. Three months ago, a plastic Santa had done me in.

It was the darndest thing, a silly accident.

I abandoned the flower arrangement and smoothed a wrinkle in the thick velvet drapes, remembering that fateful day. The sun had been out, melting away the last of the Christmas snow. I'd decided to walk over to Artie's Meats and Deli, over on Main Street, a block away from the funeral home, to grab a bite for lunch since they had the best homemade chili this side of the Mississippi. I'd just opened the door when the snow and ice around the plastic Santa Claus Artie had put on the roof of the deli gave way, sending the five-foot jolly man crashing down on my head, knocking me out.

Flat out.

I knew I was on my way to meet my maker when Chicken Teater showed up at my hospital bedside. I had put Chicken Teater in the ground two years ago. But there he was, telling me all sorts of crazy things that I didn't understand. He blabbed on and on about guns, murders and all sorts of dealings I wanted to know nothing about.

It wasn't until my older sister and business partner, Charlotte Rae Raines, walked right through Chicken Teater's body, demanding that the doctor do something for my hallucinations, that I realized I wasn't dead after all.

I had been *hallucinating*. That's all. Hallucinating.

Doc Clyde said I had a case of the "Funeral Trauma" from working with the dead too long.

Too long? At twenty-eight, I had been an undertaker for only three years. I had been around the funeral home my whole life. It was the family business, currently owned by my granny, but run by my sister and me.

Some family business.

Ruthie tugged my sleeve, bringing me out of my memories. "And her!" she said, pointing across the room. Every single one of Ruthie's fingers was filled up to its knuckles with rings. She had been very specific in her funeral "pre-need" arrangements, and had diagramed where she wanted every single piece of jewelry placed on her during her viewing. The jewelry jangled as she wagged a finger at Sleepy Hollow's mayor, Anna Grace May. "I've been trying to get an appointment to see her for two weeks and she couldn't make time for me. Hmmph."

Doc Clyde had never been able to explain the touching thing. If Ruthie *was* a hallucination, how could she touch me? I rubbed my arm, trying to erase the feeling, and watched as everyone in the room turned their heads toward Mayor May.

Ruthie crossed her arms, lowered her brow and snarled. "Must be an election year, her showing up here like this."

"She's pretty busy," I whispered.

Mayor May sashayed her way up to see old Ruthie laid out, shaking hands along the way as if she were the president of the United States about to deliver the State of the Union speech. Her long, straight auburn hair was neatly tucked behind each ear, and her tight pencil skirt showed off her curvy body in just the right places. Her perfect white teeth glistened in the dull funeral-home setting.

If she wasn't close enough to shake your hand, the mayor did her standard wink and wave. I swear that was how she got elected. Mayor May was the first Sleepy Hollow official to ever get elected to office without being born and bred here. She was a quick talker and good with the old people, who made up the majority of the population. She didn't know the history of all the familial generations—how my grandfather had built Eternal Slumber with his own hands or how Sleepy Hollow had been a big coal town back in the day—which made her a bit of an outsider. Still, she was a good mayor and everyone seemed to like her.

All the men in the room eyed Mayor May's wiggle as she made her way down the center aisle of the viewing room. A few smacks could be heard from the women punching their husbands in the arm to stop them from gawking.

Ruthie said, "I know, especially now with that new development happening in town. It's why I wanted to talk to her."

New development? This was the first time I had heard anything about a new development. There hadn't been anything new in Sleepy Hollow in ... a long time.

We could certainly use a little developing, but it would come at the risk of disturbing Sleepy Hollow's main income. The town was a top destination in Kentucky because of our many caves and caverns. Any digging could wreak havoc with what was going on underground.

Before I could ask Ruthie for more information, she said, "It's about time *they* got here."

In the vestibule, all the blue-haired ladies from the Auxiliary Club (Ruthie's only friends) stood side by side with their pocketbooks hooked in the crooks of their elbows. They were taking their sweet time signing the guest book.

The guest book was to be given to the next of kin, whom I still hadn't had any luck finding. As a matter of fact, I didn't have any family members listed in my files for Ruthie.

Ruthie walked over to her friends, eyeing them as they talked about her. She looked like she was chomping at the bit to join in the gossip, but put her hand up to her mouth. The corners of her eyes turned down, and a tear balanced on the edge of her eyelid as if she realized her fate had truly been sealed.

A flash of movement caught my eye, and I nearly groaned as I spotted my sister Charlotte Rae snaking through the crowd, her fiery gaze leveled on me. I tried to sidestep around Pastor Brown but was quickly jerked to a stop when she called after me.

"Did I just see you over here talking to yourself, Emma Lee?" She gave me a death stare that might just put me next to old Ruthie in her casket.

"Me? No." I laughed. When it came to Charlotte Rae, denial was my best defense.

My sister stood much taller than me. Her sparkly green eyes, long red hair, and girl-next-door look made families feel comfortable discussing their loved one's final resting needs with her. That was why she ran the sales side of our business, while I covered almost everything else.

Details. That was my specialty. I couldn't help but notice Charlotte Rae's pink nails were a perfect match to her pink blouse. She was perfectly beautiful.

Not that I was unattractive, but my brown hair was definitely dull if I didn't get highlights, which reminded me that I needed to make an appointment at the hair salon. My hazel eyes didn't twinkle like Charlotte Rae's. Nor did my legs climb to the sky like Charlotte's. She was blessed with Grandpa Raines's family genes of long and lean, while I took after Granny's side of the family— average.

Charlotte Rae leaned over and whispered, "Seriously, are you seeing something?"

I shook my head. There was no way I was going to spill the beans about seeing Ruthie. Truth be told, I'd been positive that seeing Chicken Teater while I was in the hospital *had* been a figment of my imagination . . . until I was called to pick up Ruthie's dead body from the Sleepy Hollow Inn and Antiques, Sleepy Hollow's one and only motel.

When she started talking to me, there was no denying the truth.

I wasn't hallucinating.

I could see ghosts.

I hadn't quite figured out what to do with this newfound talent of mine, and didn't really want to discuss it with anyone until I did. Especially Charlotte. If she suspected what was going on, she'd have Doc Clyde give me one of those little pills that he said cured the "Funeral Trauma," but only made me sleepy and groggy.

Charlotte Rae leaned over and fussed at me through her gritted teeth. "If you are seeing something or *someone*, you better keep your mouth shut."

That was one thing Charlotte Rae was good at. She could keep a smile on her face and stab you in the back at the same time. She went on. "You've already lost Blue Goose Moore and Shelby Parks to Burns Funeral Home because they didn't want the 'Funeral Trauma' to rub off on them."

My lips were as tight as bark on a tree about seeing or hearing Ruthie. In fact, I didn't understand enough of it myself to speak of it.

I was saved from more denials as the Auxiliary women filed into the viewing room one by one. I jumped at the chance to make them feel welcome—and leave my sister behind. "Right this way, ladies." I gestured down the center aisle for the Auxiliary women to make their way to the casket.

One lady shook her head. "I can't believe she fell down the inn's steps. She was always so good on her feet. So sad."

"It could happen to any of us," another blue-haired lady rattled off as she consoled her friend.

"Yes, it's a sad day," I murmured and followed them up to the front of the room, stopping a few times on the way so they could say hi to some of the townsfolk they recognized.

"Fall?" Ruthie leaned against her casket as the

ladies paid their respects. "What does she mean 'fall'?" Ruthie begged to know. Frantically, she looked at me and back at the lady.

I ignored her, because answering would really set town tongues to wagging, and adjusted the arrangement of roses that lay across the mahogany casket. The smell of the flowers made my stomach curl. There was a certain odor to a roomful of floral arrangements that didn't sit well with me. Even as a child, I never liked the scent.

Ruthie, however, was not going to be ignored.

"Emma Lee Raines, I know you can hear me. You listen to me." There was a desperate plea in her voice. "I didn't fall."

Okay, *that* got my attention. I needed to hear this. I gave a sharp nod of my chin, motioning for her to follow me.

Pulling my hands out of the rose arrangement, I smoothed down the front of my skirt and started to walk back down the aisle toward the entrance of the viewing room.

We'd barely made it into the vestibule before Ruthie was right in my face. "Emma Lee, I did *not* fall down those stairs. Someone pushed me. Don't you understand? I was murdered!"

A GHOSTLY GRAVE

**There's a ghost on the loose—
and a fox in the henhouse**

Four years ago, the Eternal Slumber Funeral Home put Chicken Teater in the ground. Now undertaker Emma Lee Raines is digging him back up. The whole scene is bad for business, especially with her granny running for mayor and a big festival setting up in town. But ever since Emma Lee started seeing ghosts, Chicken's been pestering her to figure out who killed him.

With her handsome boyfriend, Sheriff Jack Henry Ross, busy getting new forensics on the old corpse, Emma Lee has time to look into her first suspect. Chicken's widow may be a former Miss Kentucky, but the love of his life was another beauty queen: Lady Cluckington, his prize-winning hen. Was Mrs. Teater the jealous type? Chicken seems to think so. Something's definitely rotten in Sleepy Hollow—and Emma Lee just prays it's not her luck.

Just think, this all started because of Santa Claus. I took a drink of my large Diet Coke Big Gulp that I had picked up from the Buy and Fly gas station on the way over to Sleepy Hollow Cemetery to watch Chicken Teater's body being exhumed from his eternal resting place—only he was far from restful.

Damn Santa. I sucked up a mouthful of Diet Coke and swallowed. *Damn Santa.*

No, I didn't mean the real jolly guy with the belly shaking like a bowlful of jelly who leaves baby dolls and toy trucks; I meant the plastic light-up ornamental kind that people stick in their front yards during Christmas. The particular plastic Santa I was talking about was the one that had fallen off the roof of Artie's Deli and Meat just as I happened to walk under it, knocking me flat out cold.

Santa didn't give me anything but a bump on the head and the gift of seeing ghosts—let me be more specific—ghosts of people who have been murdered. They called me the Betweener medium, at least that was what the psychic from Lexington told us . . . *us* . . . *sigh* . . . I looked over at Jack Henry.

The Ray Ban sunglasses covered up his big brown eyes, which were the exact same color as a Hershey's chocolate bar. I looked into his eyes. And as with a chocolate bar, once I stared at them, I was a goner. Lost, in fact.

Today I was positive his eyes would be watering from the stench of a casket that had been buried for four years—almost four years to the day, now that I thought about it.

Jack Henry, my boyfriend and Sleepy Hollow sheriff, motioned for John Howard Lloyd to drop the claw that was attached to the tractor and begin digging. John Howard, my employee at Eternal Slumber Funeral Home, didn't mind digging up the grave. He dug it four years ago, so why not? He hummed a tune, happily chewing—gumming, since he had no teeth—a piece of straw he had grabbed up off the ground before he took his post behind the tractor controls. If someone who didn't know him came upon John Howard, they'd think he was a serial killer, with his dirty overalls, wiry hair and gummy smile.

The buzz of a moped scooter caused me to look back at the street. There was a crowd that had gathered behind the yellow police line to see what was happening because it wasn't every day someone's body was plucked from its resting place.

"Zula Fae Raines Payne, get back here!" an officer scolded my granny, who didn't pay him any attention. She waved her handkerchief in the air with one hand while she steered her moped right on through the police tape. "This is a crime scene and you aren't allowed over there."

Granny didn't even wobble but held the moped steady when she snapped right through the yellow tape.

"Woo hoooo, Emma!" Granny hollered, ignoring the officer, who was getting a little too close to her. A black helmet snapped on the side covered the top of her head, giving her plenty of room to sport her large black-rimmed sunglasses. She twisted the handle to full throttle. The officer took off at a full sprint to catch up to her. He put his arm out to grab her. "I declare!" Granny jerked her head back. "I'm Zula Raines Payne, the owner of Eternal Slumber, and this is one of my clients!"

"Ma'am, I know who you are. With all due respect, because my momma and pa taught me to respect my elders—and I do respect you, Ms. Payne—I can't let you cross that tape. You are going to have to go back behind the line!" He ran behind her and pointed to the yellow tape that she had already zipped through. "This is a crime scene. Need I remind you that you turned over operations of your business to your granddaughter? And only *she* has the right to be on the other side of the line."

I curled my head back around to see what Jack Henry and John were doing and pretended the roar of the excavator was drowning out the sounds around me, including those of Granny screaming my name. Plus, I didn't want to get into any sort of argument with Granny, since half the town came out to watch the 7 a.m. exhumation, and the Auxiliary women were the first in line—and would be the first to be at the Higher Grounds Café, eating their scones, drinking their coffee and coming up with all sorts of reasons why we had exhumed the body.

I could hear them now. *Ever since Zula Fae left Emma Lee and Charlotte Rae in charge of Eternal Slumber, it's gone downhill*, or my personal favorite, *I'm not going to lay my corpse at Eternal Slumber just to have that crazy Emma Lee dig me back up. Especially since she's got a case of the Funeral Trauma.*

The "Funeral Trauma." After the whole Santa incident, I told Doc Clyde I was having some sort of hallucinations and seeing dead people. He said I had been in the funeral business a little too long and seeing corpses all of my life had been traumatic.

Regardless, the officer was half right—me and my sister were in charge of Eternal Slumber. At twenty-eight, I had been an undertaker for only three years. But, I had been around the funeral home my whole life. It is the family business, one I didn't want to do until I turned twenty-five years old and decided I better keep the business going. *Some business.* Currently, Granny still owned Eternal Slumber, but my sister, Charlotte Rae, and I ran the joint.

My parents completely retired and moved to Florida. Thank God for Skype or I'd never see them. I guess Granny was semi-retired. I say semi-retired because she put her two cents in when she wanted to. Today she wanted to.

Some family business.

Granny brought the moped to an abrupt stop. She hopped right off and flicked the snap of the strap and pulled the helmet off along with her sunglasses. She hung the helmet on the handlebars and the glasses dangled from the *V* in her sweater exactly where she wanted it to hang—

between her boobs. Doc Clyde was there and Granny had him on the hook exactly where she wanted to keep him.

Her short flaming-red hair looked like it was on fire, with the morning sun beaming down as she used her fingers to spike it up a little more than usual. After all, she knew she had to look good because she was the center of attention—next to Chicken Teater's exhumed body.

The officer ran up and grabbed the scooter's handle. He knew better than to touch Granny.

"I am sure your momma and pa did bring you up right, but if you don't let me go . . ." Granny jerked the scooter toward her. She was a true Southern belle and put things in a way that no other woman could. I looked back at them and waved her over. The police officer stepped aside. Granny took her hanky out of her bra and wiped off the officer's shoulder like she was cleaning lint or something. "It was *lovely* to meet you." Granny's voice dripped like sweet honey. She put the hanky back where she had gotten it.

I snickered. *Lovely* wasn't always a compliment from a Southern gal. Like the gentleman he claimed to be, he took his hat off to Granny and smiled.

She didn't pay him any attention as she bee-lined it toward me.

"Hi," she said in her sweet Southern drawl,

waving at everyone around us. She gave a little extra wink toward Doc Clyde. His cheeks rose to a scarlet red. Nervously, he ran his fingers through his thinning hair and pushed it to the side, defining the side part.

Everyone in town knew he had been keeping late hours just for Granny, even though she wasn't a bit sick. God knew what they were doing and I didn't want to know.

Granny pointed her hanky toward Pastor Brown who was there to say a little prayer when the casket was exhumed. Waking the dead wasn't high on anyone's priority list. Granny put the cloth over her mouth and leaning in, she whispered, "Emma Lee, you better have a good reason to be digging up Chicken Teater."

We both looked at the large concrete chicken gravestone. The small gold plate at the base of the stone statue displayed all of Colonel Chicken Teater's stats with his parting words: *Chicken has left the coop.*

"Why don't you go worry about the Inn." I suggested for her to leave and glanced over at John Howard. He had to be getting close to reaching the casket vault.

Granny gave me the stink-eye.

"It was only a suggestion." I put my hands up in the air as a truce sign.

Granny owned, operated and lived at the only bed-and-breakfast in town, the Sleepy Hollow Inn, known as "the Inn" around here. Everyone loved staying at the large mansion, which sat at the foothills of the caverns and caves that made Sleepy Hollow a main attraction in Kentucky . . . besides horses and University of Kentucky basketball.

Sleepy Hollow was a small tourist town that was low on crime, and that was the way we liked it.

Sniff, sniff. Whimpers were coming from underneath the large black floppy hat.

Granny and I looked over at Marla Maria Teater, Chicken's wife. She had come dressed to the nines with her black V-neck dress hitting her curves in all the right places. The hat covered up the eyes she was dabbing.

Of course, when the police notified her that they had good reason to believe that Chicken didn't die of a serious bout of pneumonia but was murdered, Marla took to her bed as any mourning widower would. She insisted on being here for the exhumation. Jack Henry had warned Marla Maria to keep quiet about why the police were opening up the files on Chicken's death. If there was a murderer on the loose and it got around, it could possibly hurt the economy, and this was Sleepy Hollow's busiest time of the year.

Granny put her arm around Marla and winked at me over Marla's shoulder.

"Now, now. I know it's hard, honey, I've buried a few myself. Granted, I've never had any dug up though." Granny wasn't lying. She has been twice widowed and I was hoping she'd stay away from marriage a third time. Poor Doc Clyde, you'd have thought he would stay away from her since her track record was . . . well . . . deadly. "That's a first in this town." Granny gave Marla Maria the elbow along with a wink and a click of her tongue.

Maybe the third time was the charm.

"Who is buried here?" Granny let go of Marla and stepped over to the smaller tombstone next to Chicken's.

"Stop!" Jack Henry screamed, waving his hands in the air. "Zula, move!"

Granny looked up and ducked just as John Howard came back for another bite of ground with the claw.

I would hate to have to bury Granny anytime soon.

"Lady Cluckington," Marla whispered, tilting her head to the side. Using her finger, she dabbed the driest eyes I had ever seen. "Our prize chicken. Well, she isn't dead *yet*."

I glanced over at her. Her tone caused a little suspicion to stir in my gut.

"She's not a chicken. She's a Spangled Russian Orloff Hen!" Chicken Teater appeared next to his grave. His stone looked small next to his six-foot-two frame. He ran his hand over the tombstone Granny had asked about. There was a date of birth, but no date of death. "You couldn't stand having another beauty queen in my life!"

"Oh no," I groaned and took another gulp of my Diet Coke. He—his ghost—was the last thing that I needed to see this morning.

"Is that sweet tea?" Chicken licked his lips. "I'd give anything to have a big ole sip of sweet tea." He towered over me. His hair was neatly combed to the right; his red plaid shirt was tucked into his carpenter jeans.

This was the third time I had seen Chicken Teater since his death. It was a shock to the community to hear of a man passing from pneumonia in his early sixties. But that was what the doctors in Lexington said he died of, no questions asked, and his funeral was held at Eternal Slumber.

The first time I had seen Chicken Teater's ghost was after my perilous run-in with Santa. I too thought I was a goner, gone to the great beyond . . . but no . . . Chicken Teater and Ruthie Sue Payne— their ghosts anyway—stood right next to my hospital bed, eyeballing me. Giving me the onceover as if he was trying to figure out if I was dead or alive. Lucky for him I was alive and seeing him.

Ruthie Sue Payne was a client at Eternal Slumber who couldn't cross over until someone helped her solve her murder. That someone was me. The Betweener.

Since I could see her, talk to her, feel her and hear her, I was the one. Thanks to me, Ruthie's murder was solved and she was now resting peacefully on the other side. Chicken was a different story.

Apparently, Ruthie was as big of a gossip in the afterlife as she was in her earthly life. That was how Chicken Teater knew about me being a Betweener. Evidently, Ruthie was telling everyone about my special gift.

Chicken Teater wouldn't leave me alone until I agreed to investigate his death because he knew he didn't die from pneumonia. He claimed he was poisoned. But who would want to kill a chicken farmer?

Regardless, it took several months of me trying to convince Jack Henry there might be a possibility Chicken Teater was murdered. After some questionable evidence, provided by Chicken Teater, the case was reopened. I didn't understand all the red tape and legal yip-yap, but here we stood today.

Now it was time for me to get Chicken Teater to the other side.

"It's not dead yet?" Granny's eyebrows rose in amazement after Marla Maria confirmed there was an empty grave. Granny couldn't get past the fact there was a gravestone for something that wasn't dead.

I was still stuck on "prize chicken." What was a prize chicken?

A loud thud echoed when John Howard sent the claw down. There was an audible gasp from the crowd. The air was thick with anticipation. What did they think they were going to see?

Suddenly my nerves took a downward dive. What if the coffin opened? Coffin makers guaranteed they lock for eternity after they are sealed, but still, it wouldn't be a good thing for John Howard to pull the coffin up and have Chicken take a tumble next to Lady Cluckington's stone.

"I think we got 'er!" John Howard stood up in the cab of the digger with pride on his face as he looked down in the hole. "Yep! That's it!" he hollered over the roar of the running motor.

Jack Henry ran over and hooked some cables on the excavator and gave the thumbs-up.

Pastor Brown dipped his head and moved his lips in a silent prayer. Granny nudged me with her boney elbow to bow my head, and I did. Marla Maria cried out.

"Aw shut up!" Chicken Teater told her and

smiled as he saw his coffin being raised from the earth. "They are going to figure out who killed me, and so help me, if it was you . . ." He shook his fist in the air in Marla Maria's direction.

Curiosity stirred in my bones. Was it going to be easy getting Chicken Teater to the other side? Was Marla Maria Teater behind his death as Chicken believed?

She was the only one who was not only in his bed at night, but right by his deathbed, so he told me. I took my little notebook out from my back pocket. I had learned from Ruthie's investigation to never leave home without it. I jotted down what Chicken had said to Marla Maria, with prize chickens next to it, followed up by a lot of exclamation points. Oh . . . I had almost forgotten that Marla Maria was Miss Kentucky in her earlier years—a *beauty queen*—I quickly wrote that down too.

"Are you getting all of this?" Chicken questioned me and twirled his finger in a circle as he referred to the little scene Marla Maria was causing with her meltdown. She leaned her butt up against Lady Cluckington's stone. Chicken rushed over to his prize chicken's gravestone and tried to shove Marla Maria off. "Get your—"

Marla Maria jerked like she could feel something touch her. She shivered. Her body shimmied from her head to her toes.

I cleared my throat, doing my best to get Chicken to stop fusing and cursing. "Are you okay?" I asked. Did she feel him?

Granny stood there taking it all in.

Marla crossed her arms in front of her and ran her hands up and down them. "I guess when I buried Chicken, I thought that was the end of it. This is creeping me out a little bit."

End of it? End of what? Your little murder plot? My mind unleashed all sorts of ways Marla Maria might have offed her man. That seemed a little too suspicious for me. Marla buttoned her lip when Jack Henry walked over. More suspicious behavior that I duly noted.

"Can you tell me how he died?" I put a hand on her back to offer some comfort, though I knew she was putting on a good act.

She shook her head, dabbed her eye and said, "He was so sick. Coughing and hacking. I was so mad because I had bags under my eyes from him keeping me up at night." *Sniff, sniff.* "I had to dab some Preparation H underneath my eyes in order to shrink them." She tapped her face right above her cheekbones.

"That's where my butt cream went?" Chicken hooted and hollered. "She knew I had a hemorrhoid the size of a golf ball and she used my cream on her face?" Chicken flailed his arms around in the air.

I bit my lip and stepped a bit closer to Marla Maria so I couldn't see Chicken out of my peripheral vision. There were a lot of things I had heard in my time, but hemorrhoids were something that I didn't care to know about.

I stared at Marla Maria's face. There wasn't a tear, a tear streak, or a single wrinkle on her perfectly made-up face. If hemorrhoids helped shrink her under-eye bags, did it also help shrink her wrinkles?

"Anyway, enough about me." She fanned her face with the handkerchief. "Chicken was so uncomfortable with all the phlegm. He could barely breathe. I let him rest, but called the doctor in the meantime." She nodded and waited for me to agree with her. I nodded back and she continued. "When the doctor came out of the bedroom, he told me Chicken was dead." A cry burst out of her as she threw her head back and held the hanky over her face.

I was sure she was hiding a smile from thinking she was pulling one over on me. Little did she know this wasn't my first rodeo with a murderer. Still, I patted her back while Chicken spat at her feet.

Jack Henry walked over. He didn't take his eyes off of Marla Maria.

"I'm sorry we have to do this, Marla." Jack took

his hat off out of respect for the widow. *Black widow,* I thought as I watched her fidget side to side, avoiding all eye contact by dabbing the corners of her eyes. "We are all done here, Zula." He nodded toward Granny.

Granny smiled.

Marla Maria nodded before she turned to go face her waiting public behind the police line.

Granny walked over to say something to Doc Clyde, giving him a little butt pat and making his face even redder than before. I waited until she was out of earshot before I said something to Jack Henry.

"That was weird. Marla Maria is a good actress." I made mention to Jack Henry because sometimes he was clueless as to how women react to different situations.

"Don't be going and blaming her just because she's his wife." Jack Henry was trying to play the good cop he always was, but I wasn't falling for his act. "It's all speculation at this point."

"Wife? She was no kind of wife to me." Chicken kicked his foot in the dirt John Howard had dug from his grave. "She only did one thing as my wife." Chicken looked back and watched Marla Maria play the poor pitiful widow as Beulah Paige Bellefry, president and CEO of Sleepy Hollow's gossip mill, drew her into a big hug while all the other Auxiliary women gathered to put in their two cents.

"La-la-la." I put my fingers in my ears and tried to drown him out. I only wanted to know how he was murdered, not how Marla Maria *was* a wife to him.

"She spent all my money," he cursed under his breath.

"*Shoo.*" I let out an audible sigh.

Over Jack's right shoulder, in the distance some movement caught my eye near the trailer park. There was a man peering out from behind a tree looking over at all the commotion. His John Deere hat helped shadow his face so I couldn't get a good look, but I chalked it up to being a curious neighbor like the rest of them. Still, I quickly wrote down the odd behavior. I had learned you never know what people knew. And I had to start from scratch on how to get Chicken to the great beyond. I wasn't sure, but I believe Chicken had lived in the trailer park. Maybe the person saw something, maybe not. He was going on the list.

"Are you okay?" Jack pulled off his sunglasses. His big brown eyes were set with worry. I grinned. A smile ruffled his mouth. "Just checking because of the la-la thing." He waved his hands in the air. "I saw you taking some notes and I know what that means."

"Yep." My one word confirmed that Chicken was there and spewing all sorts of valuable information. Jack Henry was the only person who knew I was a Betweener, and he knew Chicken was right here with us even though he couldn't see him. When I told him about Chicken Teater's little visits to me and how he wouldn't leave me alone until we figured out who killed him, Jack Henry knew it to be true. "I'll tell you later."

I jotted down a note about Marla Maria spending all of Chicken's money, or so he said. Which made me question her involvement even more. Was he no use to her with a zero bank account and she offed him? I didn't know he had money.

"I can see your little noggin running a mile a minute." Jack bent down and looked at me square in the eyes.

"Just taking it all in." I bit my lip. I had learned from my last ghost that I had to keep some things to myself until I got the full scoop. And right now, Chicken hadn't given me any solid information.

"You worry about getting all the information you can from your little friend." Jack Henry pointed to the air beside me. I pointed to the air beside him where Chicken's ghost was actually standing. Jack grimaced. "Whatever. I don't care where he is." He shivered.

Even though Jack Henry knew I could see ghosts, he wasn't completely comfortable.

"You leave the investigation to me." Jack Henry put his sunglasses back on. Sexy dripped from him, making my heart jump a few beats.

"Uh-huh." I looked away. Looking away from Jack Henry when he was warning me was a common occurrence. I knew I had to do my own investigating and couldn't get lost in his eyes while lying to him.

Besides, I didn't have a whole lot of information. Chicken knew he was murdered but had no clue how. He was only able to give me clues about his life and it was up to me to put them together.

"I'm not kidding." Jack Henry took his finger and put it on my chin, pulling it toward him. He gave me a quick kiss. "We are almost finished up here. I'll sign all the paperwork and send the body on over to Eternal Slumber for Vernon to get going on some new toxicology reports we have ordered." He took his officer hat off and used his forearm to wipe the sweat off his brow.

"He's there waiting," I said. Vernon Baxter was a retired doctor who performed any and all autopsies the Sleepy Hollow police needed and I let him use Eternal Slumber for free. I had all the newest technology and equipment used in autopsies in the basement of the funeral home.

"Go on up!" Jack Henry gave John the thumbs-up and walked closer. Slowly John Howard lifted the coffin completely out of the grave and sat it right on top of the church truck, which looked like a gurney.

"Do you think she did it?" I glanced over at Marla Maria, as she talked a good talk.

"Did what?" Granny walked up and asked. She turned to see what I was looking at. "Did you dig him up because his death is being investigated for murder?" Granny gasped.

"Now Granny, don't go spreading rumors." I couldn't deny or admit to what she said. If I admitted the truth to her question, I would be betraying Jack Henry. If I denied her question, I would be lying to Granny. And no one lies to Granny.

In a lickety-split, Granny was next to her scooter.

"I'll be over. Put the coffee on," Granny hollered before she put her helmet back on her head, snapped the strap in place, and revved up the scooter and buzzed off in the direction of town, giving a little *toot-toot* and wave to the Auxiliary women as she passed.

Once the chains were unhooked from the coffin and the excavator was out of the way, Jack Henry and I guided the coffin on the church truck into the back of my hearse. Before I shut the door, I had a sick feeling that someone was watching me. Of course the crowd was still there, but I mean someone was watching *my* every move.

I looked back over my shoulder toward the trailer park. The man in the John Deere hat popped out of sight behind the tree when he saw me look at him.

I shut the hearse door and got into the driver's side. Before I left the cemetery, I looked in my rearview mirror at the tree. The man was standing there. This time the shadow of the hat didn't hide his eyes.

We locked eyes.

"Look away," Chicken Teater warned me when he appeared in the passenger seat.

A GHOSTLY DEMISE

**The prodigal father returns—
but this ghost is no holy spirit**

When she runs into her friend's deadbeat dad at the local deli, undertaker Emma Lee Raines can't wait to tell Mary Anna Hardy that he's back in Sleepy Hollow, Kentucky, after five long years. Cephus Hardy may have been the town drunk, but he didn't disappear on an epic bender like everyone thought: He was murdered. And he's heard that Emma Lee's been helping lost souls move on to that great big party in the sky.

Why do ghosts always bother Emma Lee at the worst times? Her granny's mayoral campaign is in high gear, a carnival is taking over the Town Square, and her hunky boyfriend, Sheriff Jack Henry Ross, is stuck wrestling runaway goats. Besides, Cephus has no clue whodunit . . . unless it was one of Mrs. Hardy's not-so-secret admirers. All roads lead Emma Lee to that carnival—and a killer who isn't clowning around.

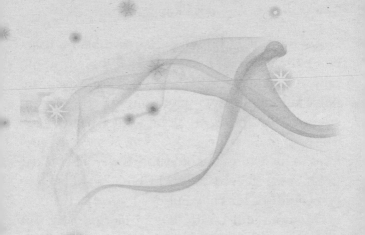

"Cephus Hardy?"

Stunned. My jaw dropped when I saw Cephus Hardy walk up to me in the magazine aisle of Artie's Meat and Deli. I was admiring the cover of *Cock and Feathers*, where my last client at Eternal Slumber Funeral Home, Chicken Teater, graced the cover with his prize Orloff Hen, Lady Cluckington.

"I declare." A Mack truck could've hit me and I wouldn't have felt it. I grinned from ear to ear.

Cephus Hardy looked the exact same as he did five years ago. Well, from what I could remember from his social visits with my momma and daddy and the few times I had seen him around our small town of Sleepy Hollow, Kentucky.

His tight, light brown curls resembled a baseball helmet. When I was younger, it amazed me how thick and dense his hair was. He always wore polyester taupe pants with the perfectly straight crease down the front, along with a brown belt. The hem of his pants ended right above the shoelaces in his white, patent-leather shoes. He tucked in his short-sleeved, plaid shirt, making it so taut you could see his belly button.

"Momma and Daddy live in Florida now, but they are going to be so happy when I tell them you are back in town. Everyone has been so worried about you." I smiled and took in his sharp, pointy nose and rosy red cheeks. I didn't take my eyes off him as I put the copy of *Cock and Feathers* back in the rack. I leaned on my full cart of groceries and noticed he hadn't even aged a bit. No wrinkles. Nothing. "Where the hell have you been?"

He shrugged. He rubbed the back of his neck.

"Who cares?" I really couldn't believe it. Mary Anna was going to be so happy since he had just up and left five years ago, telling no one—nor had he contacted anyone since. "You won't believe what Granny is doing."

I pointed over his shoulder at the election poster taped up on Artie's Meat and Deli's storefront window.

"Granny is running against O'Dell Burns for mayor." I cackled, looking in the distance at the poster of Zula Fae Raines Payne all laid-back in the rocking chair on the front porch of the Sleepy Hollow Inn with a glass of her famous iced tea in her hand.

It took us ten times to get a picture she said was good enough to use on all her promotional items for the campaign. Since she was all of five-foot-four, her feet dangled. She didn't want people to vote on her size; therefore, the photo was from the lap up. I told Granny that I didn't know who she thought she was fooling. Everyone who was eligible to vote knew her and how tall she was. She insisted. I didn't argue anymore. No one, and I mean no one, wins an argument against Zula Fae Raines Payne. Including me.

"She looks good." Cephus raised his brows, lips turned down.

"She sure does," I noted.

For a twice-widowed seventy-seven-year-old, Granny acted like she was in her fifties. I wasn't sure if her red hair was still hers or if Mary Anna kept it up on the down-low, but Granny would never be seen going to Girl's Best Friend unless there was some sort of gossip that needed to be heard. Otherwise, she wanted everyone to see her as the good Southern belle she was.

"Against O'Dell Burns?" Cephus asked. Slowly, he nodded in approval.

It was no secret that Granny and O'Dell had butted heads a time or two. The outcome of the election was going to be interesting, to say the least.

"Yep. She retired three years ago, leaving me and Charlotte Rae in charge of Eternal Slumber."

It was true. I was the undertaker of Eternal Slumber Funeral Home. It might make some folks' skin crawl to think about being around dead people all the time, but it was job security at its finest. O'Dell Burns owned Burns Funeral, the other funeral home in Sleepy Hollow, which made him and Granny enemies from the get-go.

O'Dell didn't bother me though. Granny didn't see it that way. We needed a new mayor, and O'Dell stepped up to the plate at the council meeting, but Granny wouldn't hear of it. So the competition didn't stop with dead people; now Granny wants all the living people too. As mayor.

"Long story short," I rambled on and on, "Granny married Earl Way Payne. He died and left Granny the Sleepy Hollow Inn. I don't know what she is thinking running for mayor because she's so busy taking care of all of the tourists at the Inn. Which reminds me"—I planted my hands on my hips—"you never answered my question. Have you seen Mary Anna yet?"

"Not yet." His lips curved in a smile.

"She's done real good for herself. She opened Girl's Best Friend Spa and has all the business since she's the only one in town. And"—I wiggled my brows—"she is working for me at Eternal Slumber."

A shiver crawled up my spine and I did a little shimmy shake, thinking about her fixing the corpses' hair and makeup. Somebody had to do it and Mary Anna didn't seem to mind a bit.

I ran my hand down my brown hair that Mary Anna had recently dyed since my short stint as a blond. I couldn't do my own hair, much less someone else's. Same for the makeup department.

I never spent much time in front of the mirror. I worked with the dead and they weren't judging me.

"Emma Lee?" Doc Clyde stood at the end of the magazine aisle with a small shopping basket in the crook of his arm. His lips set in a tight line. "Are you feeling all right?"

"Better than ever." My voice rose when I pointed to Cephus. "Especially now that Cephus is back in town."

"Have you been taking your meds for the Funeral Trauma?" He ran his free hand in his thin hair, placing the few remaining strands to the side. His chin was pointy and jutted out even more as he shuffled his thick-soled doctor shoes down the old, tiled floor. "You know, it's only been nine months since your accident. And it could take years before the symptoms go away."

"Funeral Trauma," I muttered, and rolled my eyes.

Cephus just grinned.

The Funeral Trauma.

A few months back I had a perilous incident with a plastic Santa Claus right here at Artie's Meat and Deli. I had walked down from the funeral home to grab some lunch. Artie had thought it was a good idea to put a life-sized plastic Santa on the roof. It was a good idea until the snow started melting and the damn thing slid right off the roof just as I was walking by, knocking me square out. Flat.

I woke up in the hospital seeing ghosts of the corpse I had buried six feet deep. I thought I had gone to the Great Beyond. But I could see my family and all the living.

I told Doc Clyde I was having some sort of hallucinations and seeing dead people. He said I had been in the funeral business a little too long and seeing corpses all of my life had been traumatizing. Granny had been in the business for over forty years. I had only been in the business for three. Something didn't add up.

Turned out, a psychic confirmed I am what was called a Betweener.

I could see ghosts of the dead who were stuck between the here and the after. Of course, no one but me and Jack Henry, my boyfriend and Sleepy Hollow's sheriff, knew. And he was still a little apprehensive about the whole thing.

"I'm fine," I assured Doc Clyde, and looked at Cephus. "Wait." I stopped and tried to swallow what felt like a mound of sand in my mouth. My mind hit rewind and took me back to the beginning of my conversation with Cephus.

A GHOSTLY MURDER

**Emma Lee Raines knows there's only
one cure for a bad case of murder**

I told you I was sick, reads the headstone above
Mamie Sue Preston's grave. She was the richest
woman in Sleepy Hollow, Kentucky, and also the
biggest hypochondriac. Ironic, considering someone killed her—and covered it up perfectly. And
how does Emma Lee, proprietor of the Eternal
Slumber Funeral Home, know all this? Because
Mamie Sue's host told her, that's how. And she's
offering big bucks to find the perp.

The catch is, Mamie Sue was buried by the
Raines family's archrival, Burns Funeral Home.
Would the Burnses stoop to framing Emma Lee's
granny? With an enterprising maid, a penny-
pinching pastor and a slimy Lexington lawyer all
making a killing off Mamie Sue's estate, Emma
Lee needs a teammate—like her dreamboat boyfriend, Sheriff Jack Henry Ross. Because with mil-
lions at stake, snooping around is definitely bad
for Emma Lee's health.

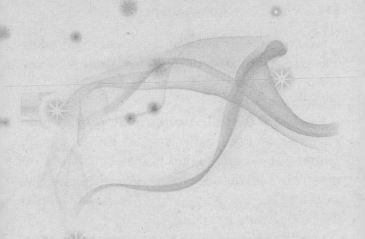

D^{*ing, ding, ding.*}
The ornamental bell on an old cemetery headstone rang out. No one touching it. No wind or breeze.

The string attached to the top of the bell hung down the stone and disappeared into the ground. To the naked eye it would seem as though the bell dinged from natural causes, like the wind, but my eye zeroed in on the string as it slowly moved up and down. Deliberately.

I stepped back and looked at the stone. The chiseled words I TOLD YOU I WAS SICK. MAMIE SUE PRESTON were scrolled in fancy lettering. Her date of death was a few years before I took over as undertaker at Eternal Slumber Funeral Home.

Granted, it was a family business I had taken over from my parents and my granny. Some family business.

Ding, ding, ding.

I looked at the bell. A petite older woman, with a short gray bob neatly combed under a small pillbox hat, was doing her best to sit ladylike on the stone, with one leg crossed over the other. She wore a pale green skirt suit. Her fingernail tapped the bell, causing it to ding.

I couldn't help but notice the large diamond on her finger, the strand of pearls around her neck and some more wrapped on her wrist. And with a gravestone like that . . . I knew she came from money.

"Honey child, you can see me, can't you?" she asked. Her lips smacked together. She grinned, not a tooth in her head. There was a cane in her hand. She tapped the stone with it. "Can you believe they buried me without my teeth?"

I closed my eyes. Squeezed them tight. Opened them back up.

"Ta-da. Still here." She put the cane on the ground and tap-danced around it on her own grave.

"Don't do that. It's bad luck." I repeated another Southern phrase I had heard all my life.

She did another little giddy-up.

"I'm serious," I said in a flat, inflectionless voice.

"Never dance or walk over someone's grave. It's bad luck."

"Honey, my luck couldn't get any worse than it already is." Her face was drawn. Her onyx eyes set. Her jaw tensed. "Thank Gawd you are here. There is no way I can cross over without my teeth." She smacked her lips. "Oh, by the way, Digger Spears just sent me, and I passed Cephus Hardy on the way. He told me exactly where I could find you."

She leaned up against the stone.

"Let me introduce myself." She stuck the cane in the crook of her elbow and adjusted the pillbox hat on her head. "I'm the wealthiest woman in Sleepy Hollow, Mamie Sue Preston, and I can pay you whatever you'd like to get me to the other side. But first, can you find my teeth?"

I tried to swallow the lump in my throat. This couldn't be happening. Couldn't I have just a few days off between my Betweener clients?

I knew exactly what she meant when she said she needed my help for her crossover, and it wasn't because she was missing her dentures.

"Whatdaya say?" Mamie Sue pulled some cash out of her suit pocket.

She licked her finger and peeled each bill back one at a time.

"Emma Lee," I heard someone call. I turned to

see Granny waving a handkerchief in the air and bolting across the cemetery toward me.

Her flaming-red hair darted about like a cardinal as she weaved in and out of the gravestones.

"See," I muttered under my breath and made sure my lips didn't move. "Granny knows not to step on a grave."

"That's about the only thing Zula Fae Raines Payne knows," Mamie said.

My head whipped around. Mamie's words got my attention. Amusement lurked in her dark eyes.

"Everyone is wondering what you are doing clear over here when you are overseeing Cephus Hardy's funeral way over there." Granny took a swig of the can of Stroh's she was holding.

Though our small town of Sleepy Hollow, Kentucky, was a dry county—which meant liquor sales were against the law— I had gotten special permission to have a beer toast at Cephus Hardy's funeral.

I glanced back at the final resting place where everyone from Cephus's funeral was still sitting under the burial awning, sipping on the beer.

"I was just looking at this old stone," I lied.

Mamie's lips pursed suspiciously when she looked at Granny. Next thing I knew, Mamie was sitting on her stone, legs crossed, tapping the bell.

Ding, ding, ding. "We have a goner who needs help!" Mamie continued to ding the bell. "A goner who is as dead as yesterday." She twirled her cane around her finger.

I did my best to ignore her. If Granny knew I was able to see the ghosts of dead people—not just any dead people, murdered dead people—she'd have me committed for what Doc Clyde called the Funeral Trauma.

A few months ago and a couple ghosts ago, I was knocked out cold from a big plastic Santa that Artie, from Artie's Meat and Deli, had stuck on the roof of his shop during the winter months. It just so happened I was walking on the sidewalk when the sun melted the snow away, sending the big fella off the roof right on top of me. I woke up in the hospital and saw that my visitor was one of my clients—one of my *dead* clients. I thought I was a goner just like him, because my Eternal Slumber clients weren't alive, they were dead, and here was one standing next to me.

When the harsh realization came to me that I wasn't dead and I was able to see dead people, I told Doc Clyde about it. He gave me some little pills and diagnosed me with the Funeral Trauma, a.k.a. a case of the crazies.

He was nice enough to say he thought I had been around dead bodies too long since I had grown up in the funeral home with Granny and my parents.

My parents took early retirement and moved to Florida, while my granny also retired, leaving me and my sister, Charlotte Rae, in charge.

"Well?" Granny tapped her toe and crossed her arms. "Are you coming back to finish the funeral or not?" She gave me the stink-eye, along with a once-over, before she slung back the can and finished off the beer. "Are you feeling all right?"

"I'm feeling great, Zula Fae Raines Payne." Mamie Sue leaned her cane up against her stone. She jumped down and clasped her hands in front of her. She stretched them over her head. She jostled her head side to side. "Much better now that I can move about, thanks to Emma Lee."

Ahem, I cleared my throat.

"Yes." I smiled and passed Granny on the way back over to Cephus Hardy's funeral. "I'm on my way."

"Wait!" Mamie called out. "I was murdered! Aren't you going to help me? Everyone said that you were the one to help me!"

Everyone? I groaned and glanced back.

Mamie Sue Preston planted her hands on her small hips. Her eyes narrowed. Her bubbly personality had dimmed. She'd been dead a long time. She wasn't going anywhere anytime soon, and neither was I.

BED-AND-BREAKFAST MYSTERIES FROM *USA TODAY* BESTSELLING AUTHOR
MARY DAHEIM

ALL THE PRETTY HEARSES
978-0-06-135159-4
Innkeeper Judith McMonigle Flynn's husband, Joe, lands in jail after his latest surveillance job abruptly ends with an insurance fraud suspect being blown away by a .38 Smith & Wesson . . . that just *happens* to belong to Joe.

LOCO MOTIVE
978-0-06-135157-0
Harried hostess Judith McMonigle Flynn decides to join her cousin Renie on a cross-country train trip to Boston on the Empire Builder. But when the train collides with a truckload of sugar beets, stranding the cousins in Middle-of-Nowhere, Montana, they soon have two murders on their hands.

VI AGRA FALLS
978-0-06-135155-6
Judith McMonigle Flynn's worst nightmare comes true when Vivian Flynn—husband Joe's first wife—moves back into the neighborhood. Vivian plans to build a big, bad condo on their idyllic cul-de-sac, attracting more than one mortal enemy. But which one ended up dead in Vivian's back yard?

GONE WITH THE WIN
978-0-06-208989-2
Judith and Cousin Renie venture into Judith's old neighborhood to track down a killer intent on seeing them come in dead last.